FROONGA
Planet

Bryan W. Fields

ILLUSTRATIONS BY
Kevan Atteberry

HENRY HOLT AND COMPANY

NEW YORK

"**A**rroooo!" Lunchbox the basset hound howled angrily from the den. Nate Parker ignored him and turned up the volume on his new CD, *Top Twenty Annoying Christmas Songs.* The dog howled again. Nate stopped untangling the tree lights and leaned inside the doorway. "Come on, Lunchbox! Show a little holiday cheer!"

"Hrrrrmmmmm," growled Lunchbox, not taking his eyes off the computer screen. He moved his fat paw slowly across the custom-made oversize keyboard designed by Nate's father.

Noyzee, he slowly typed.

"You're going to have to spell better than that if you ever want to explain how that machine works," said Nate.

"But I guess it's pretty good for a dog." He shrugged. The novelty of having a dog made intelligent by space aliens had been replaced by nonstop work. Just six months earlier, he'd helped Lunchbox build the mysterious machine that turned ordinary garbage into the world's most nutritious dog food, and narrowly avoided blowing up the planet in the process. After the Fourth of July, however, the aliens had apparently left. Aside from having the weirdest dog in the world, nothing unusual had happened—no more things disappeared in flashes of light, no more Dumpsters fell from the sky, no more garbage trucks tipped over in the parking lot.

Nate flipped through the stack of schematic drawings on the table by the computer. "Dad's figured out most of the wiring and stuff, but we really need to know what that glowing Frisbee-thing is."

Wrld eksplod, typed Lunchbox. *No tuch.*

"I *know* it could make the world explode." Nate sighed. "But *why*?"

Lunchbox let the loose skin on his forehead fold over his eyes as he tried to think. How do I explain plookie radiation? I have the whole Scwozzwort engineering library in my head, but in people talk I have the vocabulary of a baby.

Above the noise of dogs barking "Jingle Bells" on his stereo, Nate heard the front door close. He hurried into the living room to turn down the volume and greet his parents.

"Sorry we're late, sweetie," said Mrs. Parker. "Daddy was training the new employees."

"That and answering a zillion phone calls from people wanting their orders of Parker's Power Pooch Pellets," grumbled Mr. Parker. "We're selling the stuff faster than we can make it." He finished putting their coats and scarves in the hall closet. "If we can't figure out how to build more machines, we'll never catch up."

"Which means we'll never get paid." Mrs. Parker sighed as she sifted through the mail, sorting the Christmas cards from the bills. "Sometimes I wonder if I shouldn't have kept my teaching job for one more year."

"But you love this company, Connie," said Mr. Parker. "We'll manage—Mayor Carson and the other investors understand it will take a while to turn a profit. Still, we really need more of those machines." He tousled Nate's hair. "Any progress with Lunchbox?"

"Not much." Nate groaned. "I gave him a spelling test today and he got one word right."

Mr. Parker smiled. "How many bassets do you know that spell better?"

"This would be easier if the aliens would come back."

"Nate, let's not bring up the aliens again, okay?"

"But they were here! How else can you explain Lunchbox being so smart?"

"I can't, son. But I just can't believe in aliens. There has to be some other explanation—something rational—maybe a rare gene that gives him extraordinary abilities to learn."

"But you always said he was nothing but bone between the ears. Something had to have changed him."

"Well . . ." Mr. Parker hesitated, fishing for a logical statement. "Maybe I was wrong. You know, ummm . . . Albert Einstein! He flunked math when he was a kid. It took a long time for his inner genius to come out."

"Maybe he met aliens, too. Have you ever seen his picture?"

"Look, Nate, I really don't want to discuss this alien nonsense right now. There has to be a more practical answer for this. We just have to keep working on it."

"At least you'll have some time off for the holidays," said Nate. He saw his parents look at each other hesitantly. "You *are* taking time off, right?"

"Connie, have you told him?" said Mr. Parker.

"No, not yet." Mrs. Parker looked uncomfortable.

"Told me what?" said Nate.

Mr. Parker took a deep breath. "Your mother and I have to take a trip to a pet food convention in Chicago. If we're going to make this business work, we have to learn all we can and make as many contacts as possible."

"When? How long?"

"Tomorrow morning. We'll be back Christmas Eve."

"Three days?"

Mr. Parker counted silently on his fingers, mouthing the days of the week. "Yep. Three days."

"Can I come with you?" pleaded Nate.

"I wish you could, son, but we can't afford it. Until we find a way to boost production, we're as poor as we ever were. If we manage to fill the orders we've already got, we'll just about break even."

"You're just going to leave us here alone?" said Nate, briefly thinking of all-night TV and popcorn.

"Of course not," said his mother. "Aunt Nelly is coming to stay while we're gone."

"Aunt Nelly? But she's *nuts*!"

"Nate, your great-aunt is not nuts." Mrs. Parker glared briefly at her husband, who was nodding his head in agreement with Nate. "She's . . . she's a little different, but she's very sweet and she'll take good care of you."

"What's she going to think about Lunchbox?"

"You'll have to keep Lunchbox under control," said Mr. Parker. "Aunt Nelly doesn't need to know anything about his . . . um . . . you know . . ."

"Weirdness?"

Mrs. Parker finished her husband's sentence for him. "Special abilities. And don't eat too much of Aunt Nelly's fruitcake."

Nate made a sour face. "Do I have to eat *any*?"

"Only enough to be polite," said his mother. "You don't want to hurt her feelings."

"I don't wanna barf, either," said Nate.

"**A**re you sure we're in the right place?" said Frazz for the oopty-grillionth time, nervously twiddling his tentacles.

"Absolutely, *sir*," snapped Grunfloz. It hadn't taken long for him to return to his habit of making *sir* sound like an insult. "These are the exact coordinates Narzargle gave us."

Frazz looked fretfully at the scanners, which still made absolutely no sense no matter how many times Grunfloz had explained them. "Is anything out there?"

"Well, let's see, microscopic gas particles, cosmic dust, a whole lot of nothing, a couple of big asteroids, and—wait—"

"What?" Frazz fumbled to undo the knot he'd accidentally tied in his tentacles.

"One of the asteroids is moving," said Grunfloz, speaking as if this were an everyday occurrence.

"It's *what*? Ow!" Frazz had yanked his tentacles free, accidentally popping himself in the eye.

The asteroid was indeed moving, changing its course to intercept the *Urplung Greebly*. A yellow sliver of light spilled from the object, growing wider as a large section of it opened up.

"Grunfloz, I think we need to get out of here," said Frazz.

"I think it's too late," said Grunfloz. The *Greebly* shuddered and groaned as the light beam yanked it from its position and pulled it toward the opening. "And I don't think that's an asteroid, *sir*."

"What is it?" cried Frazz, his eyestalks and head tendrils turning orange.

"Hoofonoggles," muttered Grunfloz.

Frazz hurried to his quarters and returned wearing a shiny medal under his lips. "We'll be fine," he said, though the squeak in his voice said otherwise. "I'm a hero on their world."

"You don't know much about Hoofonoggles, obviously," said Grunfloz flatly. He quickly locked down all of the ship's nonessential systems. "They're just about the most obnoxious creatures in the galaxy."

"I thought that was *your* title," said Frazz, trying to calm himself.

"I said 'just about.' I can think of one more."

"Who?"

"Oogash," mumbled Grunfloz, gesturing toward the view screen. A huge Scwozzwort appeared on the screen, looking annoyed. He was even bigger and uglier than Grunfloz. In spite of the static of the comlink, his voice was intimidating, a low growl that sounded more like a sustained belch.

"*Urplung Greebly*, prepare for automatic docking. Oogash out."

Grunfloz leaned back in his couch and bobbed his

eyestalks toward Frazz. "I still can't believe you sent that report to Narzargle."

"Commander Narzargle is the one who sent us out here on this stupid voyage in the first place," said Frazz. "I thought maybe this would be a chance for redemption."

"I'm not the one who needed redemption," said Grunfloz. "You're the one with the *eebeedee* hanging over his head!"

Frazz shuddered at the mention of the official embarrassment ceremony. There was no greater punishment on Scwozzwortia than being draped in the *yakayaka*, the Robe of Stupidity, placed on a cart at the head of a long and raucous procession, pelted with rotten garbage, and then being forced to live in the streets, singing the *malfurbum gwealfee* song, begging for *froonga* crumbs the rest of his life. It was the only thing he could think of that was worse than what he had already been through.

"If it weren't for the Hoofonoggles, I'd be doing the Dance of Stupidity door-to-door," said Frazz.

Grunfloz smiled slightly. "Whatever the reason, we've had some great adventures as a result."

"If you call totally trashing the ship and putting our lives and an entire planet in danger a great adventure." Frazz reverently touched the medal. "The Hoofonoggle Medal of Generosity . . . awarded to me because I totally messed up the sales transaction when they bought the

Urplung fleet from Central Command. The Hoofonoggles got an incredible bargain, and I got banished. There was one *Urplung* ship left." Frazz frowned at the battered, grimy walls surrounding them. "Just my luck."

"And you didn't get the *eebeedee*. Sounds lucky to me."

"I have more rights as an honorary citizen of Hoofonogglia than I do on our own world," said Frazz sadly. "And I don't know anything about how to be a Hoofonoggle."

"I've dealt with the Hoofonoggles in my time," said Grunfloz. "Believe me, even your presence elevates them."

"You never told me you'd met the Hoofonoggles," said Frazz. "I thought you'd always been a hazardous garbage sorter at the central *froonga* plant."

"I also played *lob-lock* for a while." Grunfloz wiped *froonga* crumbs from his belly while picking bits from his yellow teeth. "Interplanetary league." He frowned slightly. "I don't want to talk about it right now."

The asteroid opened wider as the beam drew the *Greebly* in. Huge mechanical arms unfolded from the opening and clamped onto the sides of the ship with a bang that resonated through the hull.

Frazz yelped at the sound. Grunfloz remained silent until the docking bay pressurized, then exhaled sharply.

"Well, let's get this over with."

"We'll—we'll be fine," stammered Frazz as he adjusted his medal. Grunfloz activated the ship's main hatch. It hissed open, squeaking occasionally as the battered hinges protested.

"After you, *sir*," said Grunfloz, waving his tentacle in mock sincerity.

"Um . . ." said Frazz.

"After *you, sir!*" Grunfloz gave him a shove through the open hatch. Frazz landed face-first on the deck of the docking bay. Pulling himself up painfully, he extracted the Medal of Generosity from his mouth and readjusted it.

Grunfloz sauntered down the gangway and looked around. "I thought there'd at least be a welcoming committee."

They surveyed the vast chamber; it seemed like any ordinary hostile alien docking bay. Their eyestalks stopped moving as they gazed at the *Urplung Greebly*—the first time in fifteen years they'd seen the ship from the outside. Its hull was pitted and scarred from micrometeor impacts. Burn marks streaked from the shattered capture beam port.

Along the walls of the bay were several rows of ships, nearly identical to the *Greebly* but with strange characters painted on their hulls.

Grunfloz squinted at the writing. "I can read a little Hoofonogglian," he said. "That one there is named the *Inflamed Nostril*. And that one next to it, let's see . . .

the *Festering Eyeball Rash* . . . and that one says *Intestinal Distress*, and that one . . ."

Frazz rolled his eyestalks. "They name their ships after *annoying medical conditions*?"

Grunfloz shrugged. "Obviously loses something in the translation."

"Obviously," snorted Frazz.

A pneumatic whooshing sound made them turn around quickly. Several large yellow creatures streamed from the outer doors of the bay. Each was tall, with a many-finned, fanged head resting on broad shoulders. Muscular arms, longer than their legs, ended in webbed claws; their feet were webbed as well, slapping on the deck as the creatures hurried to surround them. Each one clutched what appeared to be a weapon.

Trying not to let his fear make him turn orange, Frazz fumbled for his medal and lifted it high for them to see. "Greetings, fellow citizens," he squeaked. The creatures stared menacingly. Tilting an eyestalk toward Grunfloz, he muttered, "I don't remember the Hoofonoggle ambassador looking like this."

"These are Hoofonoggle shock troops," said Grunfloz.

The line of creatures parted as an enormous, ugly Scwozzwort lumbered through.

"Welcome aboard," rumbled Oogash. "Commander Narzargle will see you immediately."

Grunfloz glanced at the wall of snarling guards around them. "I see your taste in friends hasn't changed much, Oogash."

Oogash looked disdainfully at Frazz, then at Grunfloz. "I see yours has gotten worse."

"Grunfloz is a loyal and efficient crew member," said Frazz. "I've referred him for several commendations."

"Of course," said Oogash with a scornful smile. "Follow me."

The Hoofonoggle guards closed ranks behind them and followed in a loose march, the uneven smacking of their feet on the deck making an unpleasant rhythm that sent chills through Frazz. They muttered unintelligible things to one another, occasionally snorting and chortling. Frazz tried to cover his nervousness by pointing to his medal and speaking to the sergeant of the guard, who marched uncomfortably close to his side.

"See this? I'm an honorary Hoofonoggle. Greetings, brother."

The Hoofonoggle scrunched his fanged mouth tight and glared sideways with his bulging eyes. "Ssshcwozz-wort, *pfleah!*" He spat a gob of something-or-other on the deck in front of Frazz.

"N-nice to meet you, too," stammered Frazz.

One by one, Nate blasted the alien ships until the TV screen was clear. He'd played this game a bazillion times, until he could almost do it with his eyes closed. As the mother ship came into view, Nate sighed and paused the game. He glanced toward the den, where his dad had closed the door to try and get some more work done at the computer.

"This is boring," he said. Lunchbox flopped on the floor next to him, yawning in agreement. Nate scratched him behind the ears. "We've already saved the world for real once. Too bad there isn't a game to help Dad's company."

Lunchbox sat up and moved to the TV screen.

"Hrrrrmmmmm," he moaned, putting a nose print in the middle of the mother ship.

"Yeah, that would be great if the aliens came back," said Nate, resuming the game and blasting the mother ship to smithereens. "But I don't think they have any reason to."

Commander Narzargle leaned across his console, which contained a mixture of Scwozzwort and Hoofonoggle technology. He moved slowly, and it was apparent that the years had not been kind to him. "I'm not going to waste time giving you a lot of details. An engineering team is repairing your ship. The Hoofonoggle fleet has a large supply of salvaged *Urplung* parts, which, thanks to your *captain*, they managed to get at a sizable discount." Narzargle rolled an eyestalk toward Frazz.

Frazz squirmed slightly. Sitting in Narzargle's presence made the *eebeedee* seem all the more likely. He fumbled for something to say in his own defense.

"Sir, about my report . . ."

Narzargle didn't answer. The door to his quarters slid open; Frazz caught a whiff of the Hoofonoggle guards outside. Oogash entered, carrying a few samples of the alien *froonga* from the *Urplung Greebly*'s cargo hold. He sneered at Grunfloz before thumping them on Narzargle's console.

"The samples you requested, sir. I've scanned them;

18

they appear to be safe." Oogash rudely bumped Grunfloz as he walked around the console to stand behind his commander.

Narzargle eyed the bricks suspiciously, then broke off a small piece and carefully placed it on his tongue. His crinkled mouth moved up and down thoughtfully. His eyes brightened for a moment, but he quickly regained control of his expression.

"Not bad," he said.

"Not *bad*?" blurted Grunfloz. "It's the best *froonga* in the galaxy!"

"I want you to take us to this *froonga* planet of yours."

"Um . . . sir?" said Frazz hesitantly. "It's kind of dangerous."

Narzargle continued looking at Grunfloz, as if Frazz didn't exist. "I'm taking command of the *Urplung Greebly*. Grunfloz, you will serve as ship's engineer."

Frazz scowled at Grunfloz, then drew himself to attention. "The *Greebly* is yours, Commander. I will be happy to serve as your first officer."

With an annoyed look, Narzargle pointed to his aide. "Oogash is my first officer."

"B–but—" stammered Frazz.

"Grunfloz, I hereby promote you to Lowly Enlisted Scwozzwort First Class."

Grunfloz put a greasy tentacle on Frazz's back. "My *captain* has already given me that designation."

Oogash bellowed in uncontrolled laughter.

Narzargle managed to contain his amusement, though he smiled smugly. "Calm yourself, Oogash. Tell me, what is the standard crew of a properly functioning *Urplung*-class ship?"

Oogash fought to regain his composure but continued chuckling under his breath. "Two officers and four enlisted crew."

"*Two* officers? Hmmm." Narzargle leaned back and folded his tentacles under his mouth. "And what are the duties of the four crew members?"

"Engineer—"

Narzargle waved a tentacle toward Grunfloz. "We've got that. What's next?"

"Navigation and cargo master."

"Hmmm." Narzargle pressed a button on his console; two burly Hoofonoggle guards rushed in, stun-zappers ready. Seeing no immediate danger, they lowered them and stared blankly at the commander.

"Admiral G'ack of the Hoofonoggle fleet has graciously assigned two of his finest troops to assist with this mission." Narzargle pointed to the shorter one. "S'pugh, which way is *up*?"

S'pugh's protruding lower fangs nearly entered his nostrils as he frowned in thought. Finally, he pointed his weapon at the ceiling and grunted.

"Good enough. You're our new navigator." Narzargle addressed the other one. "P'lak! Do you know how to count?"

The taller one smiled and nodded eagerly. Frazz could have sworn he heard something rattle.

"Looks like we're covered there," said Narzargle calmly.

"B-but, *sir*," pleaded Frazz. "What about—"

Ignoring him, Narzargle turned to Oogash again. "And the fourth position?"

"Well, Commander, *someone* has to clean the ship." Oogash grinned wickedly.

"Fine. Lowly Enlisted Scwozzwort Third Class Frazz,

have every deck on the *Greebly* spotless before we launch."

"But, *SIR!*" Frazz cried.

"Those are your orders!" barked Narzargle. "Unless, of course, you'd rather stay here with your 'honorary Hoofonoggle brothers.'"

"I look stupid," muttered Nate. Lunchbox moaned in agreement and tugged harder on the plastic wagon, which had been decorated to resemble a sleigh. The fake antlers on his head slid sideways. Aunt Nelly quickly moved to straighten them.

"You're both just adorable," she twittered, adjusting the floor-length red coat of her Mrs. Claus costume. The white fur trim matched her hair perfectly. "Nate, you make a wonderful elf! Now let's hurry. We don't want to keep everyone waiting!"

Scowling at the pointy green slippers Aunt Nelly had made him wear, Nate trudged down the office hallway as if going to his own execution. The wagon, with its load

of fruitcake, was heavy, even for a superdog like Lunch-box. Aunt Nelly swung the door to the manufacturing area wide open.

"Hello, everyone! Merry Christmas!" she cried. The employees lined up to receive their boxes of fruitcake, giggling at Nate as he pulled the green stocking cap low over his eyes.

"Hey, Nate, nice tights," teased one of the truck drivers.

"Must be pound cake," said another worker after Aunt Nelly had passed by. "Maybe ten-pound cake."

Good thing Aunt Nelly's hard of hearing. Nate grunted—the boxes *were* heavy. But then again, this was Aunt Nelly's superfruitcake, suitable for doorstops or foundation blocks, anything except eating.

Lunchbox sniffed the boxes as Nate handed them out.

This would make good *froonga*, he thought, if we softened it up first.

Stan, the gruff production manager, tucked his clipboard under his arm and clapped his hands loudly. "Thank you, Mrs. Claus, elf, and, uh . . . reindeer. Okay, people, party's over, back to work!"

"Oh, but there's still more fruitcake to give away here! Gerald told me there were thirty employees," said Aunt Nelly.

"Don't worry, ma'am, we'll save the rest of it for the second shift." Stan unhooked the wagon from Lunchbox's back and rolled it to the corner. "You guys hear that? Only one fruitcake per person. No seconds!"

"No problem," said the head garbage loader, looking at his open box and rapping the cake with his knuckles.

Freed from the wagon, Lunchbox quickly shook off the antlers and let them fall to the factory floor. Nate picked them up and headed for the men's room to put his warm clothes back on, but paused to watch the workers operate the machinery. Freshly processed dog food bricks were fed into the chopper, which cut them into bite-sized bits; a conveyor belt then dumped the green

25

chunks into the bagger, which sealed them in ten-, twenty-, and fifty-pound bags with a glossy photo of Lunchbox on the front.

Most interesting was the new automated pallet wrapper. The forklift placed full loads of dog food on a round platform, which then rotated as a mechanical arm with a roll of stretch wrap moved up and down, sealing the stacks in several layers of plastic, ready to be shipped. Lunchbox thumped his tail, always fascinated by technology.

After changing, Nate met Aunt Nelly in the hall. "What about this?" He held up the elf costume as if it were a dead rat.

Aunt Nelly pointed to the coat hooks on the wall. "Oh, just hang it up there for now. We'll come back for the second shift, if we have time." She placed her red robe on one of the hooks, patted it affectionately, and strolled toward the exit.

Second shift. Great, I get to look like a dork twice today. Nate followed her to the parking lot. Lunchbox plodded behind him, really wishing he could stay and watch the machines.

Aunt Nelly's Studebaker smelled like musty upholstery and fruitcake. A bluish cloud enveloped them as the engine coughed to life. Nate tightened his seat belt and prepared himself for another harrowing slow-motion trek across town. Aunt Nelly never took the car out of second gear and had a habit of making left turns from the right lane, but they made it home safely. Nate would have kissed the ground but the snow was dirty.

"I'm baking cookies," said Aunt Nelly. "Would you like to help me?"

"Ummm . . ." Nate made a mental note of where the kitchen fire extinguisher was, and then headed for the den. "I've got a project to work on for school." Lunchbox was already in the den; Nate quickly closed the door.

"Okay, we've got some real work to do," said Nate. He switched the computer on and opened the program with the schematic drawing of the dog food machine. Lunchbox positioned himself in front of the oversize keyboard. Nate pointed to the mysterious disk in the drawing. "Tell me what this thing is."

Lunchbox wrinkled his forehead and thought carefully. Ever so slowly, he moved his paws on the keys, one at a time.

P-R-O-O—he backspaced and started again, trying to remember the sounds that Nate had been painstakingly teaching him for the last few months. *P-L-U-U-K-E-E*, he typed.

"*Pluu-kee*," repeated Nate. "Great. It's a *pluu-kee*. I just learned an alien word. So what does it *do*?"

Lunchbox whined to himself, then typed *no wrld eksplod.*

"No world explode," Nate verified as Lunchbox wagged his tail in agreement. "I think we already knew that. *How?*"

Lunchbox flopped his head on the desk in exasperation and exhaled. Nate rolled his eyes at the ceiling. It was going to be a long afternoon.

5

Frazz leaned wearily against the cargo bay wall and sighed. Through the view port the stars streaked past, a sure sign that the Hoofonoggle technicians had successfully replaced the ship's hyperspace engines. Despite his exhaustion, he still felt like he could scream.

As if being reduced to the lowest possible rank and forced to scrub every deck hadn't been enough, he'd had to watch Narzargle move into the captain's quarters. The ultimate insult, though, was his assignment to share the cramped crew cabin with Grunfloz, who now outranked him. Frazz was certain that whatever was growing under Grunfloz's bunk was going to slither across the line he'd drawn down the center of the cabin and eat him in the middle of the night.

He looked hungrily across the cargo bay toward the *froonga* storage. His stomach rumbled. Carefully, he checked to see that no one else was around, and then crept over to the keypad.

If I'm lucky they didn't change all the command codes yet. He quickly punched the buttons with his tentacle and sighed with relief as the container hissed open. The smell of delicious off-world *froonga* made him drool. Just a small morsel.

"LOWLY ENLISTED SCWOZZWORT THIRD CLASS!" Oogash appeared in the doorway. "What are you doing in the officers' *froonga*?"

"Ummm . . . I . . . I was cleaning the hatch, sir." Frazz withdrew his tentacle and tucked it behind him.

"Ri-i-i-i-ight," snarled Oogash. He stepped closer to Frazz and glared down at him.

Frazz hung his eyestalks in shame. "I was hungry, sir. . . . There are no rations left in the crew quarters."

"That's what happens when you bunk with a *flarmgrok* like Grunfloz. But then again, *malfurbum gwealfees* are supposed to *beg* for their crumbs." Oogash smirked wickedly and turned away for a moment. Frazz cringed, knowing what was coming next.

"Sing me"—Oogash whirled around to face him again—"the *malfurbum gwealfee* song."

"Please, sir . . . *no!*"

"SING!" ordered Oogash. "It will be good practice for you."

"But sir! What about the Treaty of Roo—"

"SING!"

Frazz swallowed hard. "I'm *malfurbum gweal*—"

"LOUDER!" roared Oogash. "And do the Dance of Stupidity, too!"

Frazz shuffled his feet and waved his tentacles feebly. "I'm *malfurbum gwealfee*, won't you please feed me, I used to have a name, now I am full of shame. . . ."

Oogash leaned down into his face. "I CAN'T *HEAR* YOU!"

Frazz's voice cracked as he strained to sing louder. "TELL YOUR CHILDREN NOT TO LOOK AT MY FACE THAT'S FULL OF GOOK! *RURFROO, RURFROO*, GIVE ME SOME CRUMBS!"

"You need to improve your footwork. More lively! AGAIN!" Oogash bellowed. "With *feeling* this time!"

"Leave him alone, Oogash!" Grunfloz shouted from the entrance.

"Since when do lowly enlisted Scwozzworts give orders to the first officer?" sneered Oogash.

Grunfloz stomped up to Oogash and glared at him. "Since when have I ever cared what an officer thinks?" he demanded.

Frazz waved his tentacles. "I can vouch for that."

"Silence!" snapped Oogash. "*Malfurbum gwealfees* do not speak unless ordered to."

Grunfloz stepped closer to Oogash. "My friend is not a *malfurbum gwealfee.*"

Oogash laughed again. "Are you challenging me, Lowly Enlisted Scwozzwort?"

"Don't hide behind your rank, Oogash. You never could beat me fairly."

"Well, then, let's just forget about my rank right now and see." Oogash thrust his eyestalks forward. A hint of orange appeared at the base of his head tendrils.

"Oogash!" Narzargle came through the entrance, authoritatively waving a tentacle. "Now is not the time to settle old grudges. We have to work together on this mission."

"Yes, sir," hissed Oogash. He curled his lip at Grunfloz, but backed off a few steps.

Narzargle exhaled sharply. "We're about to arrive at the *froonga* planet. I need everyone on the bridge."

As they headed for the bridge, Oogash blocked Frazz with his huge tentacle. "Everyone except *you*, that is. Get back to work."

Nate tried to hold his breath as Aunt Nelly retrieved the fourth smoking batch of cookies from the oven. He'd made little progress with Lunchbox at the computer before Aunt Nelly drafted him to help prepare her gifts for the neighborhood.

"They're only a little scorched," clucked Aunt Nelly. "Some frosting and a few candy sprinkles and they'll be just fine." She began chipping them from the pan with her spatula. "I can't wait to share these!"

Nate forced a smile while slowly arranging what vaguely resembled Christmas cookies in one of the dozens of boxes Aunt Nelly had brought with her. Poisoning people door-to-door wasn't exactly his idea of spreading holiday cheer.

Lunchbox sniffed the full boxes stacked on the floor and made a sound that Nate assumed was the canine equivalent of *ugh*.

"And *tomorrow*," Aunt Nelly gushed, "is the Mill Ferron Fruitcake Festival. I've signed up for the fruitcake bake-off. I just *know* I'll win it!"

"This town has never seen fruitcake like yours, that's for sure." Nate sighed. Maybe with Aunt Nelly busy at the festival, though, he could stay home with Lunchbox and work on the machine mystery. He could only hope.

"We'll have so much fun there," said Aunt Nelly. "They'll have games and songs, and I hear that someone *very special* will be there." She looked down into Nate's face through her thick glasses, which magnified her eyes to the size of half-dollars. "Have *you* been a good boy this year?"

Oh, puh-leez, thought Nate. It's Amos Grubb in a rented suit, and he spits tobacco juice all over the kids when he *ho-ho-ho*'s. "Yeah, I guess so," he mumbled. If saving the world didn't count as being a good boy, nothing would.

Lunchbox looked up at Nate and whimpered, anxious to get back to work.

"I know," whispered Nate. "We're wasting time."

Aunt Nelly glanced at the kitchen wall clock. "Oh, dear, look how late it's getting."

Nate sighed with relief. Maybe he wouldn't have to wear that stupid elf costume again.

"Nate, I've got so much work to do to get ready for the fruitcake festival. Would you be a dear and deliver these goodies for me?"

"Uh . . ." Nate glanced out the window. A big snow-storm was in progress. The wind rattled the windows and pasted big flakes against the glass. He looked at Lunchbox, who wagged his tail as if he had a good idea.

"Lunchbox, are you nuts? It's really cold out there!" hissed Nate. Lunchbox nosed the boxes, then looked over at the bag of Parker's Power Pooch Pellets in the corner by his food dish. He wagged his tail again. Nate knew that look.

Aunt Nelly glanced out the window. "Oh, dear, I didn't realize it was snowing so hard. Perhaps you'd better stay home." Her face brightened. "We can watch *Frosty the Snowman* again!"

Nate quickly jumped up from the table. "Don't worry, Aunt Nelly! I can deliver those cookies, no problem." He glanced down at Lunchbox. "I have the perfect sled dog."

We've arrived at the planet, sir," said Oogash. "Orbit established."

"Excellent." Narzargle turned to S'pugh and P'lak. "Do you remember your orders?"

"Find massssheeeen," said P'lak. "Test massssheeeen. Make *froongaaaaaah*."

"Commander," said Grunfloz, "that's really a dumb idea."

Narzargle quickly suppressed the orange that appeared on his head tendrils. "Does the chief engineer have some . . . *concerns* about this mission?"

"Only that you're sending these two *narf*-brains down there instead of me."

S'pugh reached for his weapon, but Narzargle waved him off. "I believe you underestimate them, Grunfloz."

"I don't think so," snapped Grunfloz. "When I tried to brief them for the mission, both of the mental enhancers *self-destructed.*"

"You don't think they're capable?"

"If brains were energy, they wouldn't have enough to move a nanobot around a dust molecule."

"Your protest is noted. The mission will proceed as planned."

"Send me down there instead," insisted Grunfloz. "I know my *froonga* machines."

"I'm afraid that would interfere with *phase two* of the mission." Narzargle bobbed an eyestalk toward the Hoofo-noggles. "S'pugh?"

"Find creeeeature. Caaaapturrrre. Bring to sssship." S'pugh patted his stun-zapper affectionately.

Narzargle looked smug. "Frazz's report said you have . . . a *soft spot* for alien life forms. I'm afraid your presence would jeopardize the success of our mission."

Grunfloz felt a twinge of heat in his head tendrils as he thought of his four-legged friend on the planet, but made a conscious effort to keep them from turning orange. He turned to the exit. "It's a dumb idea, Commander."

As soon as he was off the bridge, Grunfloz broke into a run down the corridor. He found Frazz wearily stuffing trash and scrap parts into the disposal pod.

"Quick! Come with me!" Grunfloz wrapped a tentacle around Frazz and dragged him to the cargo bay.

"Owww! Grunfloz! I have to finish this or Oogash will make me dance again!"

"No time! Listen up! Narzargle's sending the Hoofonoggles down there to find our creature! You have to warn it!"

"Why? Why me?" cried Frazz.

"No time to explain now!" Grunfloz yanked open a Hoofonoggle equipment container and stuffed Frazz inside. "You'll have to sneak out when you get there!

When you find the creature, tell it the whole planet is in danger!"

"But—"

"Sssh! They're coming!" Grunfloz slammed the container shut just before the Hoofonoggles entered the bay.

"*Sssssshcwossssshwort!* No touch Hoofonoggle ssstuff!" snarled P'lak.

"Just making sure it's all secure, finheads." Grunfloz thumped the container with Frazz in it and smiled innocently. "Yup, ready to go. Enjoy your visit. Great planet. Yummy *froonga.*"

"*Froonga—pfleah!*" The Hoofonoggles hefted the containers as if they weighed nothing and carried them out.

"*Narf*-brains," muttered Grunfloz.

Aunt Nelly waved from the front porch. "Be careful, Nate! And thank you, dear! Hurry back!" She quickly closed the door against the blowing snow.

Nate acknowledged her, though with the scarf around his face and three layers of clothing under his parka, it was difficult to move or speak. Still, it was better than having to endure that old video again. He checked the tension on the bungee cords that held the cookies to the sled.

"Okay, Lunchbox! Mush!"

Lunchbox grabbed the sled's rope in his teeth and started pulling. The snow was too deep for his short legs, but with the strength from Parker's Power Pooch Pellets, he just plowed on through it. The sled's runners made thin tracks on either side of the rut made by Lunchbox's chest and belly. Nate followed behind the sled, occasionally stopping to tromp in knee-deep snowdrifts just for the heck of it. He shined his flashlight ahead of Lunchbox, who seemed to know where he was going with or without the light.

They cut across yards and vacant lots, making a beeline for the dog food factory.

We'll turn this stuff into *froonga*, thought Lunchbox. It's the only humane thing to do.

"**O**ogash," said Narzargle. "Confine Grunfloz to his quarters for insubordination."

"I've already set up the force field, sir." He waved Grunfloz toward the exit with mock politeness. "After you."

"Of course," said Grunfloz calmly. "Brains before ugly."

As soon as they were in the corridor, Oogash jabbed his stun-zapper into Grunfloz's side.

"I should zap you right now. Don't think I don't know what you are."

"I'm the only one you could never beat in *lob-lock* without cheating."

"*I* was the league champion!" Oogash barked. "The committee's review of your protest was flawed!" His head tendrils began turning orange. "But this isn't about that game. I know why you were assigned to this ship."

"Still sore about it, I see. Hey, it was fresh garbage—I sorted it myself! I'm sorry you weren't happy with the way the package was delivered." Grunfloz walked jauntily into his quarters, then turned to face Oogash at the hatch. "It's not my fault it exploded. See, we had this infestation of *noxplur* worms . . ."

Oogash clenched his teeth, but smiled as he engaged the force field. "This isn't over yet."

"What, you want a rematch? I can still whip you with one tentacle tied behind my back!"

"You're a fool, Grunfloz." Oogash turned and headed down the corridor toward the bridge.

"And you're a sore loser!" shouted Grunfloz, wagging his tentacles. "Loser! Nyaaaah, nyaaaaah!"

Satisfied that he had made Oogash's head tendrils turn bright orange, Grunfloz flopped onto his bunk and began thinking.

Frazz felt faint. It was dark and cramped inside the cargo container. He could hear banging, crashing, and scraping outside, and knew that the Hoofonoggles were dragging the rest of the equipment in from the platform. Gingerly he pushed at the lid with his tentacle. It was heavy, but he managed to lift it just a crack. Dim light and fresh but very cold air poured into the container. He maneuvered one eyestalk free from the tangle of equipment around him and peered through the crack. S'pugh and P'lak were standing nearby with their backs to him, surveying the area. Shivering in the cold, they hissed and growled in their language. S'pugh slowly walked around and inspected some of the other machinery. He touched a button on one, and a pallet of *froonga* began rotating while a mechanical arm wrapped a clear stretchy material around it. P'lak motioned for him to turn it off as he pulled his comlink from its holster.

"Commmaanderrrr, thissss P'lak!"

"I hear you." Narzargle's voice crackled in the comlink.

"Have come to make-*froonga* place. Massssheeeen here."

"Very well. Conduct your tests and report back. Narzargle out."

S'pugh and P'lak snarled and rubbed their webbed claws on their bodies. Clearly they were not enjoying the cold. One of them spied a door, and after much scratching, figured out how to open it. Warm air wafted from the entrance. The Hoofonoggles hurried in and closed the door behind them.

Frazz crept carefully from the container, exhaling sharply as his round feet touched the cold cement floor.

How was he ever going to find their creature friend? He wrapped his tentacles tightly around himself. It really was cold here—unlike the last time he'd come to this planet, when it was blistering hot. What a hostile environment! How could intelligent life develop in a place like this?

Frazz suddenly caught a familiar scent in the cold air. He looked around. There it was! Stacks and stacks of *froonga* bricks! Overcome by hunger, Frazz ran to the nearest stack. He stuffed a brick into his mouth and sighed blissfully. Quickly he reached for another, and another . . .

"Ssssshcwosssssshwort!"

Frazz whirled to see the Hoofonoggles, weapons drawn, glaring at him. P'lak was wearing a bright red robe with white furry trim; S'pugh had on a green sort of tunic and a matching hat. They looked ridiculous—but also dangerous.

"Oh . . . um . . . hi there!" Frazz stammered through a mouthful of *froonga*.

The Hoofonoggles looked at each other and chortled. Frazz swallowed quickly. Before he could think of something to say, long yellow arms reached out and grabbed him.

"Ow! Look, I was planning to share it! It's officers' *froonga*, the best there is! Have some!" Frazz babbled as the Hoofonoggles dragged him toward the wrapping machine.

44

"No eeeeeats *froongaaaaaaaa*," said P'lak. *"Pfleah!"* He
shoved the load of wrapped *froonga* off the rotating platform and tossed Frazz onto it. S'pugh quickly activated
the machine.

"Aaaargh! Please! I get dizzy! It'll make me *rurfroo*!
Mmmmmph!" The clear sheet wrapped itself around
Frazz's mouth as he spun. Layer after layer covered him,
tighter and tighter, until he could no longer move his
tentacles or even his eyestalks.

Laughing and grunting, the Hoofonoggles went back
to the cargo containers and began removing equipment.

Frazz watched helplessly, unable to breathe until he managed to work his tongue between a couple of layers. Unfortunately, however, his tongue got stuck and he could not pull it back into his mouth, and he had to sit there, letting the moisture on it slowly freeze, and watch the Hoofonoggles attach various diagnostic devices to the *froonga* machine.

P'lak held his long arms far away from his face as he carried a mass of rotting garbage to the input chute of the machine. S'pugh poked a button with his claw; the machine began humming and grinding. Both of them hurried to the output end and awaited the results.

Frazz watched nervously. The machine began glowing red in the center. Suddenly a bright wave of greenish light burst from the machine, a brief flash that lit up the entire area. Again, another flash, and again, faster and faster, creating a strobe effect that made the Hoofonoggles' movements seem jerky.

Frazz squinted his eyes tightly, waiting for what was surely the inevitable chain reaction that would destroy the entire planet and its neighbors, including the sun. After several minutes he opened them again. The machine was quiet. Nothing had happened, except that the Hoofonoggles were standing there arguing with each other. From the machine oozed a mass of green goo that didn't even remotely resemble *froonga*. Frazz thought about the oozy thing from Furporis Twelve for a moment, then reminded himself that it could be worse. At least this blob wasn't alive.

P'lak and S'pugh moved to their equipment and began checking the various readouts on the control panel. The squabbling continued as they moved the calibration controls back and forth, apparently unable to agree on the proper setting. Still shivering from the cold, they finally agreed to continue their argument in the warm part of the building.

Nate brushed the snow out of his eyes and wrapped the scarf more tightly around his face. Lunchbox didn't seem to mind it at all, and kept his pace right through the gate up to the loading dock. Suddenly he stopped and growled.

The lights were on! Nate checked the parking lot. No cars. Lunchbox hopped onto the icy dock, still growling, and sniffed the roll-up door. Light spilled from a burned hole where the latch was supposed to be.

"Lunchbox! Be quiet!" Nate climbed onto the dock and eased over to the hole. Peering through, he couldn't see anything unusual. But wait! Some strange objects were near the dog food machine. Wires and hoses connected a very alien-looking contraption to it.

Before Nate could think about what to do, Lunchbox pushed his nose under the door and raised it up.

"Sssh! Not so loud!" hissed Nate. Lunchbox wriggled under the door. Nate shook his head and belly-crawled behind him.

Lunchbox began sniffing around, finding strange smells that assaulted his nostrils. A mass of unidentifiable goo oozed from the end of the *froonga* machine. He followed the scents in a meandering trail around the factory. He stopped and growled near the pallet wrapper as a vaguely familiar scent mingled with the unfamiliar ones. Nate hurried over to him, trying not to let the noise of his boots reverberate around the building.

A load of full bags had been knocked off the pallet wrapper. Bags of dog food lay scattered about. On the platform was a ball of plastic that reflected the light. Something green was wrapped up, and it wasn't dog food bags. Nate and Lunchbox crept closer. It moved! Nate jumped back in terror as a shrill squeal emanated from it. It had eyeballs! One eye worked its way loose from the plastic; it looked like a giant slug eye.

An alien! Nate trembled with adrenaline. Another eye popped loose from the wrapping, and a greenish pink tongue poked through a hole in the center. Again the alien squealed. Nate backed up another ten feet, but Lunchbox trotted right up to the thing and sniffed it. The alien made some unintelligible noises; Lunchbox wagged his tail and whimpered softly.

Nate slowly stepped toward it. It was breathing in strained gasps, apparently suffocating in the plastic. The plastic around its tongue moved in and out with each desperate breath.

"Don't move," said Nate, reaching toward the plastic with his gloved hand. "I have a phaser, and I know how to use it!" He tugged at the plastic, causing the alien to breathe more rapidly. Its eyes seemed to be pleading. Nate hoped it wasn't some kind of alien mind trick, but he felt

sorry for it. He pulled his Boy Scout knife from his backpack and unfolded it. The alien trembled and whined louder.

"It's okay, it's okay." Nate carefully pulled the plastic away and cut it. The alien held its breath until Nate had finished, then scrambled backward away from him. It had two long tentacles that curled down from its sides; its mouth was huge, centered on its body. It had a definite underbite. A couple of large square teeth protruded upward from behind its lower lip. Its two feet resembled elephant or hippo feet, only rounder. Standing upright, it was about the same height as Nate. Lunchbox danced around it as if it were a long-lost friend.

Nate pointed to himself. *"Naaate,"* he said slowly. The creature stared at him blankly. *"Naaate,"* he repeated. Still no reaction. Nate had seen dozens of TV shows where aliens spoke English or communicated telepathically. Apparently TV had been lying to him all these years.

The alien acted like it had something stuck on its tongue, then slowly pointed a tentacle toward him. *"Naa-a-a-a-te,"* it rasped.

"That's right! Nate!" Nate said excitedly, pointing to himself again. Then he pointed his finger at the alien. "And you?"

The alien held its tentacles close to itself. "Fraaazz," it said.

"Frazz," said Nate. "Pleased to meet you." He waited

for some sort of response. The alien did not reply, though it seemed to relax a bit. It turned to Lunchbox and began babbling something and pointed a tentacle toward the office area, where lights were on. Lunchbox growled.

A shape appeared in the frosted glass window of the office entrance.

"Let's get out of here!" said Nate. The Frazz-thing squealed and followed behind Nate, its round feet thumping on the cold concrete. Lunchbox stood protectively at the rear, waiting to see what was coming through the door. Frazz babbled again, and Lunchbox took off running. Nate scrambled under the loading dock door and pushed it up higher so the plump alien could wriggle through. Nate leaped from the dock into the deepening snow; Frazz waddled to the edge and stood there, apparently frozen in fear. The snow was deeper than his legs. Lunchbox shoved him from behind, and the alien tumbled into the snow, flailing his tentacles.

"Run!" shouted Nate. Frazz tried to follow him through the snow, but couldn't gain any traction.

Lunchbox shoved the load of cookies from the sled and barked at Frazz, who climbed clumsily aboard and held on with his tentacles. Lunchbox grabbed the end of the rope in his teeth and began pulling. Frazz was definitely heavier than Aunt Nelly's cookies. Nate grabbed on to the rope and tugged with all his might. As they scraped the sled across the frozen parking lot, he glanced back. Through the blowing snow he saw two dim shapes on the dock. Snow suddenly sizzled and splattered around them.

"They're shooting at us! Go faster!" Nate and Lunchbox dragged the sled into the icy street, turning the corner so fast that Frazz was nearly thrown off. When they got across the town square, it was downhill for the next few blocks. Nate let go of the rope, climbed onto the sled behind the alien, and leaned over its back. In the commonsense part of his mind, a little voice told him that this was really a gross thing to do, but he shrugged off the thought as the sled coasted down the street, gaining speed.

"Lunchbox! Look out!" shouted Nate. Lunchbox kept the rope in his teeth and leaped gracefully onto Nate's back, and the three of them sailed down the hill together, with Frazz squealing in terror and nobody steering.

"**G**runfloz, I'm really disappointed in you." Narzargle stood in the corridor. The force field rippled as he spoke. Oogash stood at his side, one tentacle resting on his stun-zapper, just in case Grunfloz had any tricks planned.

"You can't imagine how much it warms my hearts to hear you say that, Commander." Grunfloz casually leaned back on his bunk.

"I cannot tolerate insubordination," said Narzargle firmly.

"Hey, everyone's got to have a hobby, you know?"

"And I suppose sending the *malfurbum gwealfee* down there to disrupt the operation is just an extension of your hobby?"

Grunfloz tried to look surprised, but inside he was very worried. Had they caught Frazz? What about the creature?

"Oh, come on, Grunfloz. Frazz would never be brave enough to do something like that on his own."

"You don't know him like I do," said Grunfloz. "Remember, we've been stuck together for over fifteen years."

"The Hoofonoggles will capture him, and the operation will continue."

Grunfloz heaved an inner sigh of relief. Frazz had escaped.

"You can't use Hoofonoggles when *plookie* radiation is involved. Anything might happen—there are too many variables. Once I saw three rookie technicians mutate right before my eyes. And that's the lucky end of the spectrum. You could destroy an entire solar system if you don't know what you're doing."

Narzargle scrunched his mouth tight in anger. "You think you know all about Hoofonoggles, don't you, Grunfloz?"

"Those two couldn't find their own noses if they looked in a mirror," said Grunfloz. "If you're thinking you can conquer that planet with a couple of dimwits like them, you're as dumb as they are."

"I don't plan on using just two of them," said Narzargle smugly.

"I didn't think so," said Grunfloz. "Let me guess, you have a whole fleet of converted *Urplung* ships stationed at the edge of this solar system, just waiting for your signal, right?"

"Something like that."

"Why? This isn't the Scwozzwort way. What's wrong with our normal procedure—you know, fair trade, peaceful relations, that sort of thing?"

"You think I should continue to head up the accounting department with a bunch of idiots like Frazz under my command?" Narzargle's head tendrils showed a hint of orange. "So I can grovel at the feet of the ultracommanders for my *froonga* rations, and labor in obscurity the rest of my life? No way!"

"So instead of working with idiots like Frazz, you choose to work with *narf*-brains like the Hoofonoggles. Yep, makes sense to me."

"Well, I happen to like the Hoofonoggle way. They're the perfect partners—they work hard, they obey orders. And *they don't eat froonga*." He folded his tentacle tips together. "Primitive, I'll admit, but your *froonga* planet has enough resources to satisfy us *and* them," Narzargle continued, clearly enjoying himself. "Enough garbage for centuries' worth of *froonga*, and enough meat to satisfy the Hoofonoggles for . . . oh, I don't know, *forever*, perhaps?"

Grunfloz rose and walked to the doorway. He stuck

his eyestalks within an inch of the force field. "Comman-der, in my professional opinion, you're totally *furmnorkle!*"

"He who controls the *froonga* supply controls Scwozz-wortia. And if anyone disagrees, they can tell it to Admiral G'ack and his battalions of Hoofonoggle shock troops."

"You don't know *snizzling gruzbunkles* about this planet's defenses," said Grunfloz. "Frazz and I barely escaped with our lives the last time we were here."

"He's bluffing, sir," snarled Oogash. "My scans have revealed no significant threat, technological or other-wise."

"Suit yourselves." Grunfloz shrugged, returning to his bunk. "I guess all of that damage to the *Greebly* was just imaginary?"

"Most likely a result of your former captain's incom-petence. There is *nothing* on this planet that can stop a spaceborne invasion," said Oogash.

"Sure. Nothing you can *see*, anyway." Grunfloz stretched and yawned. "Now, if you'll excuse me, you're interrupting my beauty nap."

Narzargle waved his eyestalks in disgust and returned to the bridge. Oogash stayed behind for a moment, glar-ing through the force field.

"*I* was the champion," he snarled.

"Good night, *loser*," said Grunfloz.

Panting, Nate opened the front door a crack and peered in. Aunt Nelly was dozing in the easy chair.

"Okay, it's clear—but be quiet!" Lunchbox stood guard on the porch while Nate carefully led the alien in by its tentacle. It was almost completely blue from the wet snow and cold, but little spots of orange were visible at the base of its head thingies. Tiptoeing, Nate took the creature into his bedroom and gestured for it to get in the closet. Frazz hesitated at the pile of dirty laundry, but quickly hunkered down when sudden screeching noises outside grew louder and closer.

Lunchbox scratched frantically at the door. Nate dashed to the living room and let him in, then quickly locked the dead bolt. Lunchbox tried to drag the hassock in front of the door, unaware that Aunt Nelly was resting her feet on it as she slept. *Thump!*

"Oh! Oh, my! I must have fallen asleep! Where are my glasses?" She fumbled around the lamp stand, accidentally knocking them to the floor.

The screeching and snarling grew louder. It sounded like a cross between a chain saw and a beginning orchestra class. Aunt Nelly rose from her chair, fiddling with the volume control on her hearing aid. Lunchbox dashed down the hall and crawled under Nate's bed.

"I knew I should have changed these batteries." She sighed. "Well, don't just stand there, Nate, unlock the door! We've got Christmas carolers!"

"Aunt Nelly! They're not carolers!"

"Nonsense, Nate, I don't need hair rollers!" Aunt Nelly pushed him aside and unlocked the door, swinging it wide open with a cheery smile. The bug-eyed aliens stared at her. Nate couldn't tell if they were surprised or if they always looked like that. They resumed howling and screeching, waving their webbed claws in the air.

"Oh, isn't it delightful, Nate? Would you get my glasses, please? I'd really like to see them better."

The aliens looked like what might result if a mad scientist tried to cross the Creature from the Black Lagoon with a yellow gorilla. The tall one wore Aunt Nelly's Mrs. Claus robe, and the short one had somehow squeezed itself into the elf costume. Nate stood frozen to the spot while Aunt Nelly started singing along.

"Oh, ho! It's great to be ho-o-o-me for the holi-da-a-a-ys!"

Nate tried to close the door, but the aliens moved up the steps. Aunt Nelly pushed it open again.

"Why, yes, of course, come in, come in! I'll get you some hot cider!"

Nate fell behind the door against the wall, knocking the umbrella stand over. One of the aliens swiveled its fin-topped head in his direction. Its companion growled and yanked its arm, and they followed Aunt Nelly into the kitchen, leaving a trail of melting snow across the floor.

"Do sit down, please!" Aunt Nelly pulled two chairs out from the table and gestured. "Go ahead! Make yourselves comfortable!"

Nate peered around the kitchen entrance, open-mouthed, as the aliens sat down hesitantly. They looked at each other and made grunting and snorting noises. The taller one seemed agitated, and thumped the shorter one.

Aunt Nelly placed china cups and saucers in front of the aliens, and then pulled a steaming kettle from the stove. She stumbled to the table and tried to focus on the cups, but poured the scalding liquid into the shorter alien's lap instead. It howled in pain and jumped up from the chair.

Aunt Nelly was delighted. "Oh, yes, please do sing another one!"

Nate moved quickly into the kitchen, grabbed Aunt Nelly's arm, and tried to pull her away.

"Aunt Nelly, we've got to get out of here!"

"Nonsense, Nate, they've got a fine ear!"

The aliens, both of them now standing, bared their fangs and howled louder.

Aunt Nelly turned to Nate. "Well, they're not professionals, I'll admit."

Nate tugged harder, and finally got her into the living room. The aliens moved toward them, pulling dangerous-looking objects from inside their coats. Then the short one stepped on the hem of the tall one's coat. Both of them slipped and fell on the polished hardwood floor.

"I WANT A HIPPOPOTAMUS FOR CHRISTMAS! ONLY A HIPPOPOTAMUS WILL DO-O-O-O. . . ." Lunchbox dashed into the room, carrying Nate's boom box in his teeth with the volume up full blast.

The startled aliens leaped to their feet and stepped back a few paces, covering the sides of their heads with their claws. All at once they ran to the front door, yanking it open as fast as they could.

With the music still blasting, Lunchbox chased them to the end of the front walk, where they slipped on the ice. One of them reached into its coat and removed a small rectangular device. Holding the object near its mouth, it snarled, and both of them suddenly shot upward and disappeared in a bright beam of light.

12

Grunfloz reached under his bunk for the receiving unit. The tiny scanner he'd stuck to the bridge bulkhead before his confinement seemed to be working perfectly. He zoomed in on Oogash, who was angrily debriefing the Hoofonoggles.

"What do you mean, 'sonic weapon'?" demanded Oogash.

"Wasssss terrrrible," hissed P'lak. He hugged the ridiculous-looking red robe more tightly around himself.

"Much paaaaaain," moaned S'pugh. "Musssssst warn Admiral G'ack."

"We've already been through this once today," muttered

Oogash. "There are no significant threats down there. Now, what about the *froonga*?"

"Massssheeeeen no work riiiight. Make oozy goo."

You finheads are in for some real surprises, Grunfloz chuckled to himself, remembering what had happened the last time he'd seen oozy goo come from a *froonga* machine.

Oogash stepped aside as Narzargle entered the bridge.

"You two are not going to make a fool of me," snapped Narzargle. "I expect you to return to the planet and complete your mission. That creature down there built that *froonga* machine; it will know the proper settings. Bring it back alive."

"That means you can't eat it," added Oogash. The Hoofonoggles looked disappointed.

"And if we can't get the information from the creature"—Narzargle smiled—"don't forget that Grunfloz is extremely fond of it. We might get his cooperation yet." Narzargle tapped his tentacles thoughtfully on the control panel. "Oh, and bring back the *malfurbum gwealfee* as well. Grunfloz seems to like him, too."

The Hoofonoggles smiled. "We torture?"

"If you behave yourselves, yes, I'll consider it."

"Only Aunt Nelly could believe this," said Nate. "And if she doesn't buy it, we're sunk." Frazz stood in the center of the bedside rug, wearing a floor-length fur overcoat that Nate had pilfered from his mother's closet. Nate's mittens tipped his tentacles, and his eyes peered out from the holes in Nate's ski mask.

Nate took a deep breath. "Here goes." He beckoned for Frazz to follow him into the living room, where Aunt Nelly was loading *Frosty the Snowman* into the VCR. Frazz hesitantly followed, trying to keep his round feet from showing under the long coat. Nate had been unable to find any galoshes in the house that would fit them.

"Aunt Nelly, this is my friend Fra—Frad—*Fred*. My friend *Fred*, and, um, his parents have to work late tonight and asked if he could spend the night here."

Aunt Nelly looked up from the VCR that flashed 12:00, 12:00, 12:00. "Well, of course he can! The more the merrier! Welcome, Fred. Take your hat and coat off and make yourself comfortable." She started to reach for the ski mask.

Nate leaned close and whispered in her ear. "He's kind of got a problem. He's really self-conscious about his looks, you see, because, he's, uh, got, um, *terminal acne*, and, um, he has to keep covered up."

Aunt Nelly looked sympathetically at Frazz. "Oh . . . oh, my. The poor child. You're such a generous boy, Nate. He's lucky to have you for a friend. Now you boys enjoy the video—the fruitcake festival is tomorrow, and I've got a lot to do in the kitchen."

Nate waited until Aunt Nelly left the room, then

quickly unplugged her ancient VCR. He hooked up his video game unit.

"This is really cool," he said to Frazz. "Watch this."

Spaceships appeared on the television screen. Nate wiggled his thumbs and proceeded to destroy them, sometimes two at a time.

Frazz watched through the mask with wide eyes. Underneath the coat his mouth flopped open in horror. He jabbered to Lunchbox—to Nate it sounded like someone playing a tape recorder backward in Swahili, but Lunchbox seemed to understand.

"Here, you try it," said Nate, handing the controller to Frazz.

Frazz held it in his mitten-covered tentacles and attempted to duplicate Nate's movements. A wave of enemy spaceships swooped in and destroyed his in a brilliant orange flash. Frazz gasped and dropped the device.

"You're dead," said Nate. He reset the game and continued, taking the fight to the enemy. He tried to forget that there really were hostile aliens out there and concentrated on the computer-generated ones that he knew he could beat. When he finally destroyed the mother ship, his thumbs were aching. Sweat beaded on his forehead. He felt no satisfaction. The real bad guys were still out there.

Bored, Lunchbox ambled to the kitchen, partly to make sure that Aunt Nelly wasn't burning it to the ground, but also because he was hungry. Over the noise of the mixer, Aunt Nelly didn't notice when Lunchbox opened the cabinet and dragged out a half-full bag of Parker's Power Pooch Pellets. He returned to the living room with the bag in his teeth and dropped it on the rug next to Nate and Frazz.

"Froonga," said Frazz. Lunchbox pushed over the bag and spilled the nuggets on the carpet. Frazz reached over and scooped up a mitten full, sticking it inside the coat and into his mouth. Lunchbox lay down on his belly and chomped away, watching the game with only vague interest. Frazz watched more intently, nervously gobbling *froonga* as if it were the last meal he'd ever eat.

Nate inserted a small thin disc into the device. "It also plays movies. This one is my all-time favorite."

Frazz's eyes widened. He almost choked on his *froonga*. Such technology! Such power! Such violence and cruelty!

"This is the best part," said Nate as the Death Star exploded and the heroes returned to their cheering comrades.

"Time for bed, boys," said Aunt Nelly, exiting the kitchen. "We've got a big day tomorrow!"

Nate tossed a beanbag chair on the bedroom floor for Frazz—it looked like it might fit his shape better than anything else. He unfolded an extra blanket for him and crawled into bed. Sleep was difficult, what with having a funny-smelling alien sitting in his room, but exhaustion eventually overtook him. Lunchbox curled up at the foot of his bed and snored.

Frazz didn't feel much like sleeping himself, not entirely convinced that he wouldn't be murdered in his sleep, or dragged off to some laboratory for weird and painful experiments. Sitting on the squishy padded thing next to *Naaaaate's* bed, Frazz wondered if he wasn't being made into a pet or something. He pulled the blanket up around himself and tried to relax. It was covered with animal hair and smelled awful.

Outside, a cold wind blew, making eerie noises and rattling the windows. The lights in the street made shadows on the wall above the bed that looked like angry Hoofonoggles. Frazz shuddered and lowered his eyestalks down to the edge of the blanket. At first he thought there was something growling under the bed, but it was only the creature snoring. At least it didn't snore as loudly as Grunfloz. Still, he moved the padded thing over to the corner, in case there *was* anything under there.

Why do I let Grunfloz talk me into these things? he wondered. No, Grunfloz didn't talk me into this; he just picked me up and stuffed me into that cargo container. Frazz glanced at the bag they'd brought in. At least I have *froonga*. He sighed, pouring himself a mouthful and chewing as quietly as possible. With his belly full, he finally fell into a fitful sleep.

"**O**h, my goodness!" cried Aunt Nelly as she emptied the fire extinguisher into the oven. "My fruitcake! What am I going to do?"

Waving the smoke toward the open window, Nate had a thought: Stay home?

Aunt Nelly's face brightened. "We'll have to go by the factory—maybe there's an extra fruitcake left over. They're best when aged a couple of days anyway."

I really don't want to go back over there, thought Nate. The aliens might be there.

The Studebaker's engine was already running as Aunt Nelly stood in the driveway. A cloud of bluish gray exhaust enveloped her in the cold morning air, but she hardly noticed it.

She waved vigorously. "Come on, boys, we're burning daylight!"

Lugging his full backpack on one shoulder, Nate checked again to make sure Frazz was bundled up properly, and led him carefully down the icy front steps and across the yard to the car. He hoped Aunt Nelly wouldn't notice the weird-looking footprints in the snow. Getting

the alien into the car was a little difficult, and not only because he was shaped so strangely and not very mobile in the long coat and mittens. It was obvious that Frazz had never seen ground transportation like this before and was hesitant to get inside.

Nate finally coaxed him in. He pulled the seat belt a little too tightly around Frazz's middle, squeezing his mouth.

"Oops," said Nate softly. "Forgot." He fastened his own seat belt. "We're ready, Aunt Nelly."

She backed the car into the freshly plowed street and then eased it forward. Little bulges distorted Frazz's ski mask as his eyestalks bobbed up and down inside it.

I hope I don't *rurfroo*, thought Frazz.

Aunt Nelly turned the car onto Industrial Street. After unpacking his Super Squirter, Nate cautiously climbed out of the car to the loading dock.

"Oh, my," said Aunt Nelly. "Are you expecting trouble?"

"You never know these days," said Nate. "Come on, Lunchbox."

Aunt Nelly smiled. "Such an imagination! Please hurry!"

Lunchbox ran ahead and sniffed the premises, barking when he determined it was all clear. Nate climbed onto the dock and returned a few minutes later with a heavy white box. He didn't tell Aunt Nelly that there were at least thirty abandoned fruitcakes still sitting in the ware-house, piled high in the green plastic wagon.

Frazz leaned over and touched a mitten-covered ten-tacle to the box in Nate's lap. *"Froonga?"*

"Afraid not," said Nate.

Lunchbox sniffed the box and growled.

"Hey, it's just fruitcake!" Nate leaned over the front seat and put the box next to Aunt Nelly. "It's not going to bite you or anything."

A large banner advertising the fruitcake festival stretched across the street just prior to the civic center's parking lot; Aunt Nelly made a quick left turn from the far right lane amid the sound of screeching brakes and honking horns. Through the holes in the ski mask, Nate saw Frazz's eyeballs squinting shut. Only when Aunt Nelly parked the car and turned off the engine did he open them.

"You get used to it after a while," said Nate. Aunt Nelly bounced from the car, bubbling with excitement. "This is going to be so much fun!" Nate made sure Frazz's disguise was in order. After adjusting the ski mask so it looked a little more like it was on a human head, he tugged on the alien's coat and led him behind Aunt Nelly into the building. Lunchbox trotted along beside them.

A man in a blue blazer met them at the door. "Sorry, son, no dogs allowed inside."

"You stay outside, Lunchbox," said Nate. Leaning

72

down, he lifted one of the dog's ears and whispered, "Watch out for aliens."

They had to stand in the registration line for several minutes before they could set up on the auditorium stage. Frazz fought the urge to run screaming in panic as the throngs of alien creatures pressed around him. He'd never felt comfortable in crowds, even among other Scwozzworts. He tried to remind himself that his new friend—at least he hoped the *Naaaaate*-thing was a friend—was apparently a mighty warrior, or at least a warrior-in-training. He wondered, however, if *Naaaaate* knew just how dangerous the Hoofonoggles could be.

"Okay, boys, we're checked in. Let's get moving!" Aunt Nelly's place was at the end of the front row. A placard with a big number seven on it matched the one pinned to the front of her dress by the registration clerk. The contestants were mostly old ladies. The winner from the previous year was Mrs. Arlene Bergstrom, a rather plump and pompous woman. She wore a gold crown and occupied the first position at the table as the reigning Fruitcake Queen, as she had for the last nine years.

Aunt Nelly glanced sideways at Mrs. Bergstrom. "Time to dethrone the queen," she said with a wry smile.

That'll be the day, thought Nate.

14

runfloz adjusted the controls on his viewer, switch-
ing from the bridge to Narzargle's quarters. Ages
ago, when Frazz had occupied the room, Grunfloz had
hidden one of his little sensors there. He hadn't used it in
a long time; spying on Frazz was really boring.

He watched Narzargle enter and sit down at the computer console.

A shriveled but still fierce-looking Hoofonoggle
appeared on Narzargle's view screen. Grunfloz turned up
the audio.

"Admiral G'ack," said Narzargle.

"Ssssssshcwossssshwort Commanderrrrr," drooled the
admiral.

"Soon to be Exalted Scwozzwort Ruler," said Narzargle. "Everything is going according to plan. Preliminary surveys of the planet are complete; it is as we suspected."

"Much *meeeeeat?*"

"This planet is crawling with, um, *resources*." Apparently Narzargle wasn't too thrilled with Hoofonoggle eating habits.

"Deeeeefenssssses?"

"It's yours for the taking."

Admiral G'ack smiled, so creepily that even Narzargle winced. "Weeeeee on our waaaay."

"Narzargle out."

Grunfloz sat up from his viewer and exhaled sharply. "Not good." He eyed the force field blocking his doorway. "Not good at all."

"This is really embarrassing," said Nate under his breath. Aunt Nelly had insisted that he and "Fred" get a chance to visit Santa Claus. She even had her camera ready.

Frazz sat uncomfortably on the red-suited hairy creature's lap, petrified with fear.

"Ho, ho, ho! Ho-o-o-o, you're a stout one." Santa grunted. The beard was real, but it was greenish yellow right under his lips.

A little boy tugged on Nate's pant leg and pointed to Frazz.

"Is that your bruvver?"

"Umm . . . no," said Nate, not looking down.

"He's *ugly*," said the boy.

None of the children waiting in line were over six years old. Nate felt like a giant. He just knew everyone was staring at him . . . and at Frazz, of course.

"You're a little shy, aren't you?" Santa Grubb chuckled. "What's your name?"

Frazz began to tremble. These creatures were really starting to weird him out. The milling crowds, the noise—it all seemed too much like the *eebeedee*.

"His name is Fred," said Nate. "He's from . . . uh . . . *Japan*."

"Oh," said Santa. "Umm . . . they got Christmas there?"

"You're Santa, you tell me," growled Nate. He felt a sudden push from behind.

"Go on, Nate, I want to get a picture of you and Fred with Santa." Aunt Nelly pointed to Santa's free leg. "Go ahead, sit down!" She raised her camera. "This is just so adorable!"

At the bright flash from Aunt Nelly's camera, Frazz squealed and fell backward onto the floor. When he came to, a red-robed figure stood over him. Slowly, his eyes focused again.

"Sssssshcwossssshwort!"

"Eeeeeeeeeee!" shrieked Frazz. "Hoofonoggle!"

"Look, Mommy, it's the Grinch!" shouted a little girl. The children crowded around the aliens, giggling and squealing.

"Hey, buddy, ya wanna get outta the picture here?" shouted Amos Grubb. "It ain't Halloween!"

"Frazz!" shouted Nate. He waded through the crowd of laughing children, brandishing his Super Squirter. The tall alien hissed at Nate and reached inside the red robe for its weapon. Nate squeezed the trigger, thankful that he'd just changed the batteries. He hit it square in the face; the alien shrieked and clutched its eyes. Nate was also thankful he'd decided to load the gun with Aunt Nelly's apple cider vinegar instead of tap water. He quickly turned and fired at the short alien. It screamed and gurgled as a jet of liquid went right up its nostrils.

The crowd scattered in confusion as mothers tried to round up their children. Aunt Nelly looked up from her camera, bewildered.

"Oh, my goodness," she said, looking at her watch. "It's time for the sing-along!" She hurried toward the auditorium. "Now where did those boys run off to?"

Nate yanked Frazz up by his coat sleeve. "We've got to get out of here!"

"I'll make sure you get a big lump of coal this year, kid!" shouted Amos Grubb.

The aliens were staggering around blindly, when suddenly the Mill Ferron High School Marching Ferrets came banging and crashing through the double front doors, the brass blasting out "I'm Gettin' Nuttin' for Christmas." Marching four abreast, the band plowed through the cheering crowd and filed into the auditorium.

The aliens covered their heads and cowered by the wall. The crowd fell in behind the band, some of them singing along.

Nate dragged Frazz into the crowd and followed them into the auditorium. The band members, still blowing their brains out, clumsily formed ranks on the stage. Hiding alongside the bass drum, Nate pushed Frazz up the side steps. The bass drummer nearly fell off the stage as they shoved past, but continued pounding, almost in time with the rest of the band.

Frazz's head reverberated painfully with each beat. What sort of torture was this creature intending? He stumbled up the steps, falling flat on his face more than once.

"Come on!" Nate struggled to help the plump alien up. "This way!" He led him around the back curtains, which were made of heavy black fabric that hung from the rafters to the floor. Though the stage floor still shook, the curtains managed to muffle the band a little bit.

Behind a large screen at the rear of the stage was the table with all the fruitcakes. The smell of sweet fruitcake ingredients was so thick in the air Nate could hardly breathe. He looked around. Security seemed a bit lax—

probably because everyone was out singing along with the band. There were about two dozen samples lined up on the long table. Each fruitcake baker in the contest had her own style. Some cakes were stacked in layers; others had been baked in bundt pans, resembling large nut-covered glazed doughnuts. Some had candied pineapple slices on them. Most of them looked edible, with the exception of Aunt Nelly's, which sat at the right end of the table, mounted on a glass cake stand that was a little higher than the others. He wondered how many people might die of food poisoning after sampling her nut-covered glazed foundation brick. He glanced at the other end of the table, where Mrs. Bergstrom's fruitcake sat amid a ring of shiny garland, perfectly colored, perfectly shaped, perfectly edible, with a circle of delicious-looking red cherry halves on top. As he wondered what real fruitcake actually tasted like, a movement in his peripheral vision made him turn back to Aunt Nelly's entry. Her fruitcake had started to sag a little on the cake stand. It looked like an invisible force was squashing it down. The cake slowly drooped down past the edge of the plate on one side. Suddenly it flopped onto the table, landing with a soft plop.

Poor Aunt Nelly, thought Nate. She'll be devastated when she loses—*whoa*! He gasped and jumped back from the table. The cake had *moved*! He watched in shocked fascination as the cake stretched itself up and down a few times, and then proceeded to slosh across the table to the next fruitcake in line, a lemon-scented creation that was a little smaller than most of them. Frazz poked his eyeballs through the holes in the ski mask and squealed in fright. Aunt Nelly's fruitcake slowly wrapped itself around the lemon cake until it had completely engulfed it. Nate heard a faint sucking sound, like someone squeezing a sponge, and then Aunt Nelly's fruitcake moved off, leaving the lemon cake looking much like it had before, but dry and slightly discolored. It moved onto the next one and did the same thing.

"Geez!" blurted Nate. The thing moved from one plate to the next, including Mrs. Bergstrom's entry. When it finished, the bright red cherries that had adorned the top of the cake looked like raisins, or maybe large rodent droppings. Indeed, a horrible smell wafted from the table as all the cakes suffered the same fate. Bloated and apparently satisfied for the moment, Aunt Nelly's cake slithered back onto its stand, gurgling and burping quietly.

Nate felt sick. An alien invasion seemed more likely than ever now. Trust no one, he told himself, not even *fruitcakes*!

He heard footsteps and hurriedly dragged Frazz behind the back curtains. The judges were coming! Two rich-looking women and a short, bearded man stepped around the tables. The man was carrying a tray that held several plastic forks, three water glasses, and a stack of napkins.

"We'll just go down the line," said the richest-looking woman. Starting at the left end, she took a fork from the short man's tray and carefully plunged it into the first cake in the row. "Napkin, please, Hector." She placed a thin slice on a napkin and sniffed it. Her eyes watered slightly. "Oh, my," she said, trying to maintain her dignity. The second woman took the slice from her and tasted it. She made a sour face and shook her head. "Next," ordered the first woman. She made the bearded man taste the next one. He coughed the piece into his napkin and wiped his mouth. "Ugh" was all he managed to say before taking a big swig of water. They moved on, choking and spitting, as they tasted one unpalatable cake after another. Twice the man had to leave to refill the water glasses.

By the time they reached Aunt Nelly's fruitcake, the judges looked very pale and shaky. Noticing that it seemed plump and moist instead of dry and shriveled like the others, and feeling too sick to taste any more, they conferred briefly. The ladies nodded grimly. The man then yanked a blue ribbon from his coat pocket and tied it around the base of Aunt Nelly's cake stand.

"Good enough," he croaked, then clutched his hand over his mouth. The judges dashed to the restrooms; only Nate saw Aunt Nelly's fruitcake jump from the table and scoot out the side door.

"Like I don't have *enough* weird stuff to worry about already," he said breathlessly. "*Nobody's* gonna believe *this*.

Come on, Frazz!" Nate pulled his squirt gun from his backpack again and dashed out into the snow, with Frazz waddling after him.

What an insane planet, Frazz huffed to himself. Who in their right minds would want to conquer this place? Brrrr! His bare feet crunched through the frozen white stuff as he tried to keep up with the *Naaaaate*-thing.

"Barrrooooo!" Lunchbox came running around the side of the building, sniffed Frazz, and plowed ahead to catch up with Nate.

"You were supposed to watch for aliens, meathead!" Nate scolded. "Follow that fruitcake!"

It rolled into the hedgerow that separated the civic center park from the town square. Lunchbox put his nose to the ground and followed its track, zigzagging through the bushes. The fruitcake burst out of the bushes and across Main Street toward Knutson's Bakery.

"Don't let it get in there!" shouted Nate. Aunt Nelly's fruitcake bumped against the door, apparently sensing goodies inside. Before Lunchbox could get to it, it squished its way through the mail slot, leaving only a gooey ring of glaze around the edges.

Frazz shuddered, remembering the oozy thing from Furporis Twelve and the mayhem that had followed. He hoped this new life form's mother wouldn't show up.

Nate shoved on the door; it was dead-bolted. A note from Mr. Knutson was taped to it. He had closed the shop to attend the fruitcake festival and would be back later that day. Lunchbox growled in frustration and pawed at the door. Nate pressed his face to the glass and watched in horror as the fruitcake crashed through the display cases. It promptly began attacking innocent gingerbread men, chocolate Yule logs, doughnuts, and sugar cookies. As each confection shriveled, the fruitcake grew, knocking over cake stands and baking pans in its search for more.

Nate's mind raced to think of a plan. The fruitcake wallowed in a large tray of crushed nuts, clearly enjoying itself as much as a pig in a mud bath. After coating itself completely, it headed for the pans of frozen bread dough Mr. Knutson had left out to thaw. Instead of merely sucking them dry, however, it completely absorbed the soft dough into itself, almost doubling its size in a matter of seconds. Then it headed for the kitchen, disappearing from Nate's sight, though he could still hear metal clattering and glass breaking.

"The back alley!" cried Nate. "Let's go!" The three of them ran around the block. Lunchbox charged ahead again. When Nate and Frazz got to the alley, Lunchbox had his ear pressed against the back door of the bakery, listening carefully. Nate brandished the Super Squirter, trembling so much that the vinegar in the bubble-shaped reservoir sloshed. Frazz stood behind Nate and twiddled his tentacles—the mittens had fallen off somewhere in the snow.

I really, really, really, really, *really* hate this planet, Frazz fumed. If I ever see Grunfloz again I'll—

Lunchbox leaped back from the door just before it banged open. The fruitcake, now the size of a truck tire and sporting a layer of squashed jelly doughnuts, crashed out into the alley. Nate fired a stream of vinegar at the monster. Little bits of soggy cake with nut fragments fell off one spot, but the fruitcake kept moving.

"Don't let it out of the alley!" shouted Nate. Lunchbox barked and snapped at it, leaping out of the way when it tried to whack him with an elongated part of itself. Jelly and soggy dough splattered on the icy pavement.

"Frazz!" Nate gestured for the alien to block the fruitcake's escape.

"Goojat zama furmnorkle?" babbled Frazz, remaining behind Nate.

"Come on, you big green weenie!" Nate grabbed Frazz by his coat sleeve and pushed him into its path. "We've got it surrounded now!" The fruitcake lunged at Frazz; Nate fired the squirt gun again, knocking off another small chunk of soggy cake that fizzed on the pavement. "Lunchbox! Cover me!" While Lunchbox distracted the fruitcake for a moment, Nate yanked a snow-covered slat from a discarded wooden pallet and took a swing at it, knocking a loose jelly doughnut into the wall. As the doughnut slid down the brick to the ground, the fruitcake rolled toward it, trying to reabsorb it. Nate knocked several icicles loose with the slat; they fell into the soft fruitcake, making little holes that quickly sealed themselves up.

"How do we kill this thing?" shouted Nate.

Frazz wrapped a tentacle around Nate's arm and tugged on it. *"Naaaaate!"*

"Not now, I'm busy!" Nate dropped the wood and took aim with the squirt gun again.

Frazz yanked Nate hard, pulling him away from the fruitcake, which suddenly exploded into a million smoking pieces, spraying a rainbow of goo all over them, as well as all over the walls and pavement.

"What the—"

"*Hoofonoggle!*" shrieked Frazz.

Nate whirled to see the two nasty aliens advancing slowly, their weapons drawn. The one wearing Aunt Nelly's red coat aimed its weapon at Frazz; a beam of light struck him right in the middle and he fell limply to the ground. The second alien leveled his weapon at Nate; Lunchbox leaped in front of Nate and caught the beam in his chest, landing on the pavement with a sickening thump.

"Lunchbox!" screamed Nate. The aliens licked their jowls and hissed as they approached. Nate raised his Super Squirter and emptied the rest of the vinegar into their faces. They screamed and clawed at their eyes but kept moving toward him. Nate backed away toward the wall. The aliens raised their weapons again, hissing and breathing heavily. They seemed to be having trouble focusing after being shot with the vinegar.

Nate snatched a glob of fruitcake goo and threw it at the short alien, knocking its elf hat off. "Take that, you dog killer!"

The tall one suddenly dropped its weapon and clutched its head. The short one reached into its tunic to retrieve its rectangular communication device, but suddenly fell to the ground and began convulsing wildly. The object clattered on the pavement and bounced several feet away. Nate watched in disbelief as a third eye appeared in the tall one's forehead. The alien screamed in agony. The other one howled as a new arm began popping out of its shoulder, ripping right through the elf costume.

Nate looked at his squirt gun. He had no idea Aunt Nelly's vinegar was that strong! Still writhing in pain, the aliens staggered to the spot where Lunchbox and Frazz had fallen. The tall one screamed into its communication gizmo. Before Nate could get to his dog, the aliens, Frazz, and Lunchbox all disappeared in a bright flash of light.

"Nooooooo! Lunchbox!" Nate screamed. He curled up in a ball on the ground and pounded the snow with his fists. "Arrrrrrgh!" For several minutes he sat there, sobbing, with ice melting into the seat of his pants.

Finally, he disassembled the squirt gun, dumped the last few drops of vinegar into the snow, and stuffed the gun into his backpack. He wiped the sticky fruitcake crumbs from his clothes with a handful of snow and took a last look around the alley. It was then that he noticed the alien object. It looked like some kind of gold-colored metal. He picked it up with his gloved hand. It had a tapered end, like a handle, big enough to wrap large webbed claws around. Mounted above the handle were several buttons beneath a smooth, rectangular area. It was fairly light; the handle seemed to balance the weight of the rest of it. He turned it over and around a few times and touched one of the buttons. Nothing happened. He stuffed it in his pack and headed back to the civic center.

15

Grunfloz lounged on his bunk, snickering at the images from the bridge.

"Aaaaaaaarrrrrrrrrrrgh!" The Hoofonoggles writhed on the floor of the capture bay. Oogash and Narzargle stood in the hatch, staring in disbelief at the mutations taking place.

"What happened?" roared Oogash.

P'lak struggled to speak as another eyeball formed on his head. Now that he had two mouths, it was difficult to control the echo.

"Fearrr-fearrrr-some-some wea-wea-pon-pons-s-s-s! Aaa-Aaa-rgggh-gggh!"

S'pugh waved one of several new arms. The one on

the top of his head stuck straight up. "Aliensss ssshooot mutaaaaaation gun, sssspray, gaaaaaaahhhhh!"

"Why didn't we know about these weapons?" demanded Narzargle. "Oogash! Initiate bioscan and decontamination; see if we can stabilize these mutations. Then I want you to do a thorough analysis of this planet's defenses . . . *again*."

"Yes, sir," grumbled Oogash. He slammed the hatch shut, pressed a few buttons, and squinted as a bright purple light bathed the Hoofonoggles and their stunned captives.

"Priceless," said Grunfloz. "This is why you don't mix *plookie* radiation and morons." He watched patiently as the decontamination proceeded. The "all clear" light came on; Oogash opened the hatch and stepped carefully inside. Grunfloz zoomed in on the Hoofonoggles, who lay panting on the deck. Something rumpled and furry slumped nearby, and next to it was—Grunfloz took a deep breath—the creature!

"This is not good," he said. The rumpled thing stirred and slowly sat up. It carefully removed its fur covering. Grunfloz felt a twinge of relief. Frazz! He was alive.

Oogash nudged the nearest Hoofonoggle with his foot—well, it looked more like a kick than a nudge.

"Can you function?" he barked.

P'lak rolled his several eyes around. There was a big one right in the center of his chest. His tongues flickered out of his mouths; a third one flopped out of his ear. "We-we-fun-fun—" He stopped and clamped his claw over one mouth. "Weeee fine."

S'pugh stretched his head-arm up to a support beam overhead and yanked himself to his feet, flexing all his new appendages mightily. A hungry smile spread across his suddenly larger mouth, showing even larger teeth. "Weeee verrrry fine."

"Wonderful," said Oogash dryly. "Take that *malfurbum gwealfee* and lock him up with the other one."

S'pugh frowned. "No eeeeeeeat?"

"Not yet."

S'pugh used three arms to grab Frazz. With a fourth one he reached for the still unconscious creature.

"Leave that one there for now," said Oogash. "We'll deal with it later." He led them down the corridor to Grunfloz's quarters.

"You have company." Oogash unlocked the force field and moved aside to let S'pugh bowl the prisoner into the cabin. Frazz rolled to a stop against Grunfloz's bunk.

"Welcome back," said Grunfloz. He waited until Oogash's laughter faded down the corridor. "It was getting a little dull around here."

"Grunfloz," whispered Frazz, stealing a glance at the mutant Hoofonoggles guarding the door. "What happened to *them*?"

"Hmm? Oh, *that*. The extra arms and eyeballs and

stuff—I knew that would happen if they messed with the *plookie* calibrations." He looked carefully at Frazz. "Looks like you're still in order. How'd you manage that?"

"I don't know—I was wrapped up in some kind of packing material when they ran the machine. Maybe it blocked the radiation?"

"Could be—it doesn't normally penetrate inorganic stuff—but just the same, you'll want to count your tentacles now and then. And if you're going to mutate, do it on your side of the room."

"So what happens now?"

"Well, they have the creature. They don't need me anymore—and I *know* they don't need you."

"You mean they're going to kill us?"

"Probably." Grunfloz fished around under his bunk for old *froonga* crumbs.

"So why don't they just do it and get it over with?"

"I don't know. . . . I suspect it has something to do with Oogash and his ego."

"You mean he wants to do it slowly and painfully so he can gloat."

"Something like that."

Frazz flopped onto his bunk across the room and tried to breathe deeply. He twiddled his tentacles.

"I assume you have a plan, Grunfloz?"

"Aaah . . . *nope.*" Grunfloz yawned for a moment. "Sounds like you had an interesting visit."

"It was a total nightmare and I nearly froze to death, but at least I had some good *froonga*." Frazz licked his lips and sighed. "Sorry I didn't bring you any."

"Narzargle's going to use the Hoofonoggles to enslave the planet and harvest its garbage. The only way any Scwozzwort is going to get some is to pay through the eyestalks for it." Grunfloz lay flat on his back and looked at the ceiling. "This is my fault."

"It's not all your fault, Grunfloz. Well, then again, it was your idea to pick up life forms from all over the galaxy, and they ate all of our *froonga*, and we nearly died, and almost blew up the planet, but—"

"Everyone needs a hobby," said Grunfloz. "It kept my mind off my failure."

"What failure? You were obviously assigned to the *Greebly* to drive me *furmnorkle*. And I think you succeeded."

"I never told you," mumbled Grunfloz. "I couldn't."

"Couldn't tell me *what*?"

"It was top secret."

"We're about to die. It's not like I'm going to *tell* anybody."

Grunfloz sat up slowly. "When you processed that order to sell forty-three *Urplung* ships to the Hoofonoggles, Narzargle was suspected of tampering with the contract. The Hoofonoggles paid the full price for the ships, but Narzargle used you to cover it up. Central Command was only paid the amount shown in your files, and Narzargle took the rest."

Frazz eyed his Medal of Generosity, which he'd left on his bunk while cleaning the ship. "You mean . . ."

"I was assigned to the *Greebly* because it was assumed you were working with Narzargle and Oogash; that you were going to rendezvous with them somewhere in space. I was sent to spy on you."

Frazz sat numbly, unable to think of anything to say.

Grunfloz folded his tentacles and continued. "I had an emergency transponder with a coded homing signal. I was supposed to activate it when we caught up with Narzargle."

"But you never did."

"No, I never did. After a while it was pretty clear that you were clueless, and that we were on a wild *gargafron* chase."

"Why didn't you contact Central Command? You could have spared me fifteen years of torture!" Frazz said bitterly.

"I couldn't. I had no way to prove you were innocent. You would have gotten the *eebeedee* anyway for stealing the *Urplung Greebly* and going on an unauthorized mission. Narzargle wanted to get you as far away from home as possible to cover his own tracks."

"I'd have been willing to take my chances," snorted Frazz. "You could have called them."

"I couldn't use the open communications channel. It was too dangerous; Narzargle might have been monitoring it—he did get your report, you know."

"You could have used that emergency *transpooder* thing. They'd have caught up with us, found us in the middle of nowhere, and I'd have had a chance to plead my case."

"I couldn't." Grunfloz hung his eyestalks in shame. "I lost it."

"You *lost* it?"

Grunfloz looked at the ceiling, trying to avoid Frazz's angry gaze. "You remember the specimen I picked up from that mountaintop on the third moon of Znood-forp?"

Frazz thought for a moment, trying to pick out the memory from hundreds of unpleasant ones he'd experienced with Grunfloz's hobby. "You mean the giant acid-spitting pimple slug that exploded in the service duct? How could I forget that!"

"Yeah, that was the one. . . . Well, it *ate* my transponder . . . so I decided to just enjoy the mission after that. I never expected to have any contact with the home planet again, and I was fine with that. I might have gotten the *eebeedee* myself." Grunfloz flopped onto his back again. "I'm sorry I never told you."

Frazz lifted his Hoofonoggle Medal of Generosity and stared at it. "I can't believe it. All this time I thought I was a hero to the Hoofonoggles. I met the Hoofonoggle ambassador!" He waved the medal in the air. "What about the Treaty of Roogah?"

Oogash suddenly appeared at the entrance, bellowing with laughter. *"Roogah,"* he roared, "was the name of my pet *flarmgrok* when I was just a *larva*! Only you would believe such a feeble disguise." He turned off the force field and entered, followed by Narzargle and the Hoofonoggles. It was suddenly very crowded; Frazz scooted back onto his bunk to protect his breathing space.

"I suppose you've come to kill us now," said Grunfloz casually.

"That would be a good idea," said Narzargle. "The sooner, the better." He turned to leave, but Oogash held up a tentacle.

"With all due respect, sir, what about 'settling old grudges'?"

Narzargle sighed wearily. "Yes, I guess now would be as good a time as any."

"May we use the cargo bay?"

"Fine, just don't make a big mess. We'll need lots of room for *froonga*."

"Aaaaannnd *meeeeeat*," said P'lak, licking his lips with all of his tongues, including the one that protruded from his ear.

"Umm . . . yes, of course," said Narzargle, looking a

little disgusted. "Now if you'll excuse me, I have an invasion fleet to contact. Don't drag it out too long, Oogash."

Grunfloz sat up again and leveled his eyestalks at Oogash. "You still can't beat me."

"Famous last words," Oogash sneered. "You'll eat them before you die."

"Do I want to know what kind of horrible torture you're discussing here?" said Frazz, tying his tentacles in knots.

"The game," said Grunfloz. "Oogash wouldn't dare let me die without playing one last game."

Oogash grinned wickedly. "Prepare yourself, Grunfloz. We'll do it in the cargo bay, after I feed your sniveling friend here to the Hoofonoggles."

"Eeeeee!" said Frazz, covering his eyestalks so he wouldn't have to look at multiple drooling tongues.

"Wait!" Grunfloz leaped to his feet. "You can't do that!"

"What, you care about this *malfurbum gwealfee*? The one you were sent to *spy* on?" Oogash held up a tentacle to stop the advancing Hoofonoggles.

"The one who's a better *lob-lock* player than either of us could ever hope to be," said Grunfloz. "You'd never beat us in a *doubles* match."

Oogash laughed hysterically. "That's rich, Grunfloz! A doubles match! Hahahahahaha!"

"I guess you'll never know, will you?" Grunfloz set his lower lip defiantly.

Oogash looked at Frazz, then at the Hoofonoggles. "Fine! Hahahaha! Doubles it is! S'pugh! P'lak! Prepare the cargo bay! We're going to have a little *tournament*!"

The Hoofonoggles grumbled, but obeyed. Oogash exited and locked the force field. "We'll be back soon. Better get to work on your game plan."

Frazz watched them leave, open-mouthed. "Grunfloz! I don't know anything about—"

"Ssssh!" Grunfloz clamped a tentacle over Frazz's mouth. "I'm trying to buy you some time! *You* just became a champion *lob-lock* player. Act the part!"

"But I don't know anything about *lob-lock*! I'm an accountant! Now we're not just going to die, we're going to get beaten to a pulp before we do!"

"Relax, I'll think of something."

"You're *furmnorkle*," said Frazz.

16

Nate slumped on the couch, staring sullenly at the Christmas tree. All afternoon he'd been trying to figure out the alien gadget, to no avail. Aunt Nelly sat in the recliner, looking very satisfied as the kids in the video constructed Frosty. Nate glanced her way.

"Your crown is bent," he said.

"Yes, well, that Bergstrom woman wouldn't let go of it."

"Not until you twisted her fingers backward, anyway."

"At least the firemen were able to restrain her before she hurt herself, the poor thing."

"Your fruitcake is definitely . . . *different*," said Nate.

"Yes . . . and someone ate it all, apparently. But the

blue ribbon was on *my* plate," she said triumphantly. "It must have been just *irresistible*."

The doughnuts certainly didn't put up much of a fight, thought Nate. He pulled a sofa cushion into his lap and wrapped his arms around it, gazing at the floor.

Aunt Nelly fished the remote from under the cushion and paused the tape. "You shouldn't worry about Lunchbox, Nate. I'm sure he'll come home. He always does, doesn't he?"

Nate blinked back a tear. "I don't think he's coming back this time."

"Well, let's go look for him, then." She started to get up from the chair.

"I've, uhh, looked everywhere already. Besides, it's pretty slick out there right now. You don't want to be driving tonight."

"Yes, I suppose it is a little too icy for my old car." Aunt Nelly sighed and resumed playing the video. "Shall I make some popcorn?"

Nate fought the urge to gag. "No, thanks."

They watched in silence for a few minutes, while the children tried to think of a name for the snowman. As usual, Aunt Nelly chuckled when the smallest one said "Oatmeal."

"Do you believe in luck?" asked Nate.

"I believe in *never giving up*," said Aunt Nelly, pausing the video again. "That's the only real luck in this world.

You'll never win them all, but you'll win enough." She patted the crown on her head. "Just because somebody won nine times, didn't guarantee she'd win the tenth time, too. I've been making fruitcakes for over forty years, and I always give it my best. But I never won anything until today. I got lucky because I never gave up."

Somehow this wasn't very comforting. "Thanks, Aunt Nelly. I'm going to bed now."

"Good night, Nate. I'll wait up in case your dog comes home. We can start looking first thing in the morning."

"Happy Birthday," said Frosty. Aunt Nelly twittered at her favorite line in the show.

Never give up. Yeah, right. Nate trudged to his room, put on his pajamas, and flopped onto the bed. Aunt Nelly didn't win because her fruitcake had finally gotten better after forty years of trying; she won because it came to life and ate all the others!

Aliens. I actually had an alien here for a sleepover. Nate tried to picture going back to school in January, assuming the world would survive until then. "Hey, Nate, I got a bike!" "Hey, Nate, I got all the Bionicles!" "Oh, yeah? I met an alien and he spent the night in my room and we got chased by alien bad guys and they blew up my great-aunt's fruitcake and stole my dog!" The smartest dog in the world. . . . He saved my life. He saved the world once. Who's going to save the world now?

17

"**I**'m *never* going to get this! We're as good as dead!" Frazz wrung his eyestalks in frustration. "Why didn't you just let them kill me and get it over with?"

"Because this game is our best chance to survive. There's a whole planet down there that is depending on us to save it, even if they don't know it."

"But we can't beat Oogash—look at the size of him! And he's in a lot better shape than you are. And the Hoofonoggles—it doesn't matter which one he partners with, one of them alone could rip us to shreds! Look how many arms they have!"

"You worry too much," said Grunfloz. "Now, let's review the basics. What is the object of the game?"

"Ummm . . . you try not to get killed?"

"Come on, be serious! We're running out of time!"

"Umm . . . you get the *bzzt*-ball, and, ummm . . ."

"And then you have to get rid of it before . . . ?" Grunfloz tried to coax the answer out of Frazz.

"Before it zaps you and locks up all of your muscles and your opponent throws you against the wall."

"Exactly. And how do you get rid of the *bzzt*-ball?"

"Ummm . . . don't tell me, I know this . . . umm . . ." Frazz squinted his eyes shut as he thought. "In one-on-one *lob-lock*, you throw it at your opponent and try to knock him out . . . and in doubles, umm, you, you try to hit an opponent with it, or, um, throw it to your partner and let him try. Is that right?"

"Close enough," said Grunfloz. "And if you miss?"

"The *bzzt*-ball fires its thrusters and tries to zap you instead."

"And then you have to dodge, and not try to catch it because it will automatically lock you, unless it bounces off the wall or your opponent first. Got that?"

"No, but keep going," said Frazz. "It's not going to matter because we'll get killed anyway."

Grunfloz ignored Frazz's whining and continued. "How do you score?"

"When your opponent gets locked . . . umm . . . and you throw him against the wall, you, uh, run to his goal and shout the best insult you can think of. The computer will score it from one to five points, but you have to do it before your opponent recovers."

"And if he recovers?"

"He gets to knock you senseless with the whacky stick thing, and he gets three points."

"It's called a *whomp-sting* stick. And if he misses?"

"You get two points."

"How do you win?"

"By, uh, *not getting killed*?"

Grunfloz rolled his eyes. "You win by scoring more points than they do before the *bzzt*-ball deactivates."

"This is a *really* dumb game," said Frazz.

"Maybe, but I *love* it. I've got a whole bunch of great new insults for Oogash."

"You're weird, Grunfloz."

The force field suddenly blinked off. Oogash poked his eyestalks into the hatch. "Rise and shine, losers! It's time to play." Oogash emphasized the word *play*, his voice low and rumbling.

Grunfloz tugged on Frazz, who had wrapped his tentacles around the support on his bunk and refused to let go.

"Come on, champ, time to teach these *gargafrons* a lesson."

"What, *how to splatter an undersized Scwozzwort against the wall*? I think they know that one! Let me go!"

Oogash snorted with amusement. "An *expert* player, hmm?"

"Come on, Frazz, we don't need to lull them into a false sense of security, do we?" Grunfloz gave a mighty yank, loosening Frazz's grip, and dragged him into the corridor, where the mutant Hoofonoggles waited to escort them to the cargo bay. He turned to Oogash. "I'm assuming you have all of the equipment we'll need."

"Packed a complete set before we left home. Official League regulation. It's my most prized possession."

"Mine is my *championship trophy*," said Grunfloz. "The one I won fair and square." He glanced over at Frazz, who was turning orange from top to bottom.

The cargo bay had been cleared of containers, except for the large *froonga* storage units, which had been pushed against the wall. Two goals had been erected, one at each end of the bay, with their insult display panels glowing slightly. In the center of the bay sat a round object with lots of points sticking out, looking like an Oogachakan spiny ball-fish. It hummed slightly, occasionally emitting little hisses from its flexible spines.

Oogash opened the equipment case and tossed a pair of *whomp-sting* sticks to his opponents. They were long, with a flat paddle shape at one end and what looked like a low-power stun-zapper nozzle at the other. Frazz picked up the stick with trembling tentacles.

Oogash then gave them the remaining pieces of equipment.

"What's this?" cried Frazz, holding it up by its straps.

"Thruster belt," said Grunfloz. "You'll need it to get around the court."

"What—we're not allowed to walk or run?"

"No. Everyone knows that *lob-lock* is played in zero-gravity."

"You didn't tell me that!" Frazz sputtered. "You know it'll make me *rurfroo!*"

"Just shut up and get your gear on."

"What about safety equipment? Helmets, pads, safety nets? Cushions on the walls?"

"I thought you said he was a champion," Oogash sneered.

"He's quite the joker, he is," said Grunfloz. "Aren't you, Frazz?" Silently he mouthed *say yes.*

"Umm . . . hehe . . ." said Frazz. Oogash waved a tentacle at S'pugh. Frazz noticed that both of the Hoofonoggles were wearing thruster belts and holding *whomp-sting* sticks, as was Oogash.

"Grunfloz," whispered Frazz, "I thought this was a doubles match—why are there thr—"

"We're playing by Hoofonoggle rules, apparently." Grunfloz set his jaw and held his weapon firmly.

"You didn't tell me about Hoofonoggle rules!" hissed Frazz.

"They're just like Scwozzwortian rules, but with two exceptions."

"And those are . . ."

"One, the winners get to eat the losers. Two, Hoofo-noggles *cheat*."

"What! *Aaaaaaaah!*" Everyone began floating as S'pugh switched off the gravity in the cargo bay. Frazz tumbled end over end, trying to buckle his thruster belt into place.

The *bzzt*-ball slowly moved into the exact center of the room. Its hundreds of spines extended and retracted as its thrusters adjusted its position.

"Are you ready?" said Oogash.

"Bring it on," said Grunfloz.

From both goal units, a computerized voice spoke. "Team Grunfloz, insult, please."

Grunfloz looked at Frazz. "This is to see who gets the first throw."

"Oh." Frazz was still tumbling. "How fun."

Grunfloz extended his eyestalks toward Oogash. "Your mother was a *flarmgrok!*"

"That was powerful," huffed Frazz. "NOT!"

"Team Oogash, insult, please," said the computer.

Oogash grinned wickedly. "Frazz is a *malfurbum gwealfee.*"

The computer beeped again. "Possession to Team Oogash."

"Don't worry, Frazz, I always like to start on defense." Grunfloz engaged his thruster belt and began slowly moving toward the far wall. Frazz turned his on and slammed his bottom painfully onto the floor; he was wearing the thruster upside down.

The *bzzt*-ball zipped across the room to Oogash's waiting tentacles. Without hesitation he whipped it toward Frazz, who had now bounced toward the ceiling. The ball connected immediately with his head and vacuumed itself on. Frazz felt a jolt through his body as his muscles locked

up. Oogash nodded his eyestalks to P'lak, who flew over to Frazz, grabbed him with his lower left arm, and with his thruster fully engaged, flung him at the wall. Frazz bounced hard, seeing stars. P'lak quickly grabbed on to the Team Grunfloz goal unit and, placing a claw on the pad, shouted something that sounded like *"Glrph ssshhoom ploomjuaaaaah."* The computer translated the insult: "'Grunfloz is very untidy.' Five points, Team Oogash."

Frazz's muscles relaxed, though his head throbbed. "That's not much of an insult! How'd they get five points?"

"Must have lost something in the translation," muttered Grunfloz.

Frazz tried to turn his thruster around; it sent him careening into the ceiling. "Ouch! *We're going to get creamed, aren't we?*"

The *bzzt*-ball reset itself and zoomed toward Grunfloz.

"Get in position! It's our turn now!" Grunfloz caught it with one tentacle, spun around three times, and sent it flying so fast that Oogash couldn't block it with his stick. It struck him square in the belly, latched on, and delivered its paralyzing shock. Oogash drifted backward, his eyes unblinking. Grunfloz tucked his eyestalks in and rammed full speed, catching Oogash just above the mouth and shoving him against the wall. "Hurry, Frazz! Get to the insult pad!"

Frazz tried to aim his thruster, and with tentacles flailing, tumbled toward Oogash's goal. The Hoofonoggles moved to block him, but Grunfloz shot between them and knocked them both out of the way with one swing of his stick. Frazz managed to loop a tentacle onto the pad and opened his mouth, but nothing came out.

"Come on Frazz, we need an insult! Before Oogash recovers!"

"Umm . . . Oogash . . . Oogash eats *flarmgrok* pus!"

The computer beeped. "Three points, Team Grunfloz."

"Only three!" shouted Frazz indignantly. "What could be grosser than *flarmgrok* pus?"

"Not bad for a first try," said Grunfloz. "Now, time to play some defense!"

The *bzzt*-ball made its way to S'pugh; he caught it with the arm that extended from the top of his head and flung it at Frazz. Grunfloz reached out with the paddle end of his stick and deflected it; the ball reset itself and zoomed back to S'pugh, who now had so many arms that it made him a pretty large target. It hit him in the chest and locked on with several of its spines.

Grunfloz moved to slam him into the wall, but S'pugh flicked the *bzzt*-ball away as if it were a *droob* fly.

"It didn't zap him!" cried Frazz.

Grunfloz changed course to avoid a vicious swipe from the Hoofonoggle's claws. "I was afraid of that! The mutation has made them zap-resistant!"

"Look out!" Frazz yelled. The *bzzt*-ball whooshed up behind Grunfloz and caught him in his head tendrils; he went stiff immediately. Oogash smiled and waved P'lak to the insult pad while he grabbed Grunfloz by one rigid tentacle and spun him into the ceiling with horrible force. Grunfloz bounced off and then hit the floor, bouncing again into the wall, so hard that even Oogash winced.

P'lak clawed the insult pad. *"Sssssnnnnirrrrrk wamza floooooogahrongaaaaa!"* he roared triumphantly.

"'Oh my, you didn't gargle this morning, did you?'" chirped the computer merrily. "Five points, Team Oogash."

Grunfloz groaned painfully, but shook himself alert. "Frazz! If that happens again you need to block him! Give me time to recover!"

"Me? Block *him*? Fine! You got a portable photon cannon?"

Grunfloz ignored him and caught the ball again. He held it for a few seconds longer, grabbing Frazz by one tentacle and towing him toward Oogash. He let the ball fly just in time. As Oogash went rigid, Grunfloz flung Frazz as hard as he could.

"Slam him, Frazz! I'll do the insult!"

The Hoofonoggles again moved to intercept. P'lak, with his fourteen or so assorted eyes watching every corner of the court at once, aimed for Frazz, while S'pugh went after Grunfloz. Frazz, unable to slow his velocity, closed his eyes and pointed his *whomp-sting* stick out in front of himself. It hit P'lak in his largest eye. The mutant howled in pain as Frazz drove him backward, slamming both him and Oogash into the wall.

Grunfloz parried S'pugh's flailing arms repeatedly as he tried to get to Oogash's goal, finally managing to get his tentacle tip on it. He took one last swipe at the Hoofonoggle with his stick and shouted his insult: "If you had an extra brain, it would be lonely!"

Ding! "Five points, Team Grunfloz."

"Yes!" whooped Grunfloz, shooting away from the snarling Hoofonoggle who now had the *bzzt*-ball in his claws. S'pugh faked a throw toward Grunfloz, then spun and whipped it into Frazz, who let out a frightened "eeep!" just before he went stiff. Oogash, who had just come to, passed him to P'lak, who was licking his injured eye with one of several long tongues. P'lak vengefully tossed Frazz by his head tendrils against the *froonga* storage locker. The door to the officers' rations bent at the impact, breaking the hinges and allowing fresh *froonga* bricks to float freely about the cargo bay.

Oogash flew to his opponents' goal. "My turn," he snarled. "Grunfloz is so ugly he has to sneak up on his own *rurfroo!*"

Ding! "Four points, Team Oogash."

Oogash frowned, sure it was worth five, but waved his

stick at Grunfloz and gloated. "Get used to it, loser! You can't beat me!"

Frazz pulled his bruised head tendrils out of the *froonga* compartment, stretching them until they popped free of the bent hatch. "I have a question, Grunfloz. If I die, does the game end?"

"Nope. They'll just keep slamming your lifeless little body into mush and scoring more points each time."

"*That's* why you love this game so much! Listen, Grunfloz, if you don't think of some way to win, we are going to be Hoofonoggle dinners—and totally tenderized!"

Grunfloz didn't answer, having once again been caught off-guard by the *bzzt*-ball. P'lak slammed him while S'pugh sped to the insult pad. Frazz, remembering what Grunfloz had said, tried to intercept him, but was zapped by Oogash's *whomp-sting* stick.

S'pugh gave a screeching, grating insult that sounded like he was chewing rocks.

"Nanny nanny boo-boo," sang the computer. "Five points, Team Oogash."

unchbox opened his eyes slowly. The capture bay of the *Urplung Greebly* gradually came into focus. He lay still, checking to make sure he was alone. His ears detected movement outside the chamber. He heard muffled voices. Carefully he crept near the door and pressed his ear to it.

"—that there are absolutely no threats to your invasion fleet, Admiral."

"Exsssssssplaaaaaain thissss report from your Hoofonoggle crewwwww."

"What report? I didn't authorize any report."

"My trooooops aaaaalwaaaays staaaay in touch. My orrrrrderrrrss."

"Yes, of course. To what are you referring?"

"Sssssssonic weaponssssss. Mutaaaaaaation sssspraaaays."

"Well, Admiral G'ack, it's a noisy planet. Be sure your forces have hearing protection and they'll be fine. As for the mutations, we haven't concluded what caused them, but we have ruled out anything from the planet. Our analysis of the supposed mutation chemical found that it's merely a fermented vegetable fluid. And the mutations have not affected their ability to perform their duties; in fact, they have been enhanced in unique ways. They should prove most useful in combat."

"Issss haaaaard to trussssst Sssssshcwosssssshwort Commanderrrrr."

"Admiral, you wound me. Have I not been in complete cooperation with you for over fifteen years? Did I not procure an entire fleet of ships for you? I repeat: *There are no significant threats on this planet.* It is yours for the taking. *Froonga* for us, meat for you."

"Weeee proceeeeeeeed. If wronnng you paaaaay big."

"Trust me, Admiral. Narzargle out."

Lunchbox slumped to the deck. The little whiny animal had mentioned a threat, but nothing like this! Hoofonoggles. He mentally searched the information the big smelly animal had downloaded into his brain. *The Encyclopedia of Everything Else* was sorely lacking in details about them except to mention that they were often very stupid. Still, he'd seen enough to know how dangerous they were.

They're not getting my *froonga*. And they'd better not eat my people, especially the ones that make the *froonga*. Lunchbox scanned the chamber. The little whiny animal's coat lay nearby. He walked over and sniffed it. He could smell the alien, as well as traces of his boy.

My boy! He sat down for a few moments and mentally reviewed the *Urplung Greebly*'s schematics, and then wagged his tail slightly. It might work, but first he had to figure out a way to get out of the capture bay.

Lunchbox studied the hatch. Of course! He scratched at the metal and barked. Nothing.

"Arrooooooo!" he howled. Usually after a good long howl someone would open the door for him. He backed up as footsteps grew closer. A pair of angry eyeballs appeared at the window. Lunchbox wagged his tail and made his sad puppy face. The eyeballs at the window disappeared; he heard a grumbled Scwozzwortian curse. Suddenly he felt a jolt through his body. Bright lights popped in his head and he nearly passed out. The stungrid! That definitely was not a nice alien out there.

Lunchbox gathered his strength and moved until he was standing on the fur coat. From the far side of the capture bay he had a better view of the window. The alien glared at him. Lunchbox howled again, louder this time, and with a few snarls thrown in for good measure. He heard the circuits pop as the alien repeatedly tapped the stun-grid button, but the coat insulated him from the floor. He kept making noise until the alien finally opened the door and stepped in, holding a stun-zapper.

The Scwozzwort was old and moved a little too slowly. Lunchbox sprinted past before the alien could fire the weapon. He skidded to a halt outside the hatch, leaped up, and hit the stun-grid button himself. The alien's eyestalks straightened as current arced between them. Lunchbox saw him fall flat on his face just as the hatch closed. He merrily wagged his tail as he trotted toward the communications panel. Standing on his hind legs with his front paws on the panel, he poked a few buttons with his nose. The coordinates of the previous transmissions flashed on the screen in bright Scwozzwortian characters. He clumsily moved his paw on the controls and selected one.

Half-asleep, Nate heard a muffled beeping sound. It was coming from his backpack on the floor by the bed. He tore the pack open and pulled out the alien gadget. The smooth, empty area glowed, shimmered briefly, and then a picture appeared.

"Lunchbox!" The image was clear, better than anything he'd seen on any Earth screens.

"Arroooo!" said Lunchbox.

"You can see me?"

"Arf!"

"What are you doing? Where are you?"

Lunchbox adjusted the picture so that Nate could see the bridge of the spaceship.

"Cool!"

Lunchbox readjusted the view so Nate could see his face again. He turned his head sideways and growled at something.

"What?" cried Nate.

Lunchbox looked at the screen and off to the side again. Quickly he leaped onto the panel and put his nose right against the screen. With his tongue he slurped the screen in a series of distinct strokes.

Nate watched in fascination as the slobber trail became visible. Crude-looking letters glowed on the screen in his hand.

"*G . . . a . . . m . . . Gam?*" Nate furrowed his brow. "What's a *gam?*"

Three more letters formed as Lunchbox licked the middle part of the screen. *P . . . l . . . a . . .*

"*Gam pla?* What the heck is that?"

Lunchbox continued writing with his tongue. *Wrld sav.*

Gam pla wrld sav. Nate wished Lunchbox could spell better. Of course! His biggest problem was with vowels— especially the silent ones!

"Gam pla wrld sav," said Nate. "Game play world save!"

Lunchbox barked happily, then looked to the side again. The screen went dark.

"Wait! Lunchbox! What does this mean?"

The door to the capture bay suddenly hissed open. A hot stun-beam flashed across the panel, just missing Lunchbox.

Oops! Time to go! Lunchbox dashed from the bridge with the alien commander shuffling after him.

Whew, that was close. Lunchbox crawled carefully through the service duct. He could hear the alien commander ranting on the bridge behind him. He closed his eyes for a moment, trying to visualize the ship's layout. *Let's see, I make a left here, and then go right. . . .*

The ducts were narrow, designed to accommodate a service robot, not a Scwozzwort. Lunchbox noted that the ducts were dirty; obviously they hadn't run a service robot through here in a long time. The only visible light came from small blinking units placed at various intervals along the way. He would have to use his nose more than his eyes. At one point along the duct the metal was rough, corroded, and somewhat crumbly, as if acid had been splashed. A little farther along, his nose bumped against a small metal box. It was corroded, with a button in the center. When his nose pressed against the button, it moved. The box emitted a high-pitched beeping sound. Lunchbox backed away, thinking it might be a weapon of some kind, but after waiting for several minutes, he moved on. Must have been a leftover piece of diagnostic equipment from years ago, he concluded. The duct opened into a small chamber. Three other passages branched off from there. Lunchbox confidently headed into the center one. About ten feet into the tube, he bumped against something round, lumpy, and hard. It was blocking the entire duct.

A rock. There's a big rock in my way. Who put a *rock* in here? He tried to shove the object with his head, but it wouldn't move. He growled in frustration.

He closed his eyes and tried to think, but a crackling, squishy sound interrupted his thoughts. He looked at the rock again. It was breaking apart! Lunchbox backed away carefully. Chunks of the rock fell off, pushed out by a . . . a *bony snout*! This wasn't a rock; it was some kind of egg! Piece after piece broke away, until a wet, shiny six-legged hairy reptilian-crustacean thing staggered out. It had scales and claws. A little bit of matted fur clung to the top of its head and back. When it opened its mouth, he could see a long, sticky tongue nestled between four little tusks. When closed, the tusks came up through little holes in its

beak. Hissing, the thing clambered toward him, flicking its gooey tongue. It opened its mouth again and let out a faint but high-pitched honk that hurt Lunchbox's ears.

He tucked his tail and backed out of the tube as quickly as possible. The thing stumbled after him, honking and squeaking. Lunchbox scrambled out into the chamber, leaped into an adjacent duct, and ran for his life.

"**G**ame play world save . . . game play world save . . ."
Nate repeated the phrase over and over. What did
Lunchbox mean? What kind of game could save the
world?

He turned the alien device over in his hands, hoping
there wasn't anything on it that would contaminate him
and make him grow extra eyeballs or something. There
were strange symbols on the buttons. He had pressed a
few of them, but nothing had happened. He examined it
more closely to see if any of the buttons were significantly
different than the others—maybe one that would switch
the thing on. Frustrated, Nate slammed the handle on his
nightstand. The screen suddenly flashed on, displaying

rows of alien characters. He tapped the base of the handle again; the screen turned off.

"Okay. Now what do I do?" He switched it on again and looked at the screen. "Here goes nothing." He pressed the first button on the left. A row of characters in the middle of the screen changed color; the others disappeared. The screen shimmered for a moment, and an ugly alien face appeared. It looked like one of the yellow reptile-gorilla aliens, but more wrinkled and angry-looking, if that were possible.

"S'pugh snasha grzlt foom?" said the alien.

"Whoa!" Nate quickly switched the device off. "Wrong number." The object vibrated in his hands and beeped loudly; the screen lit up again to show the same alien, this time peering intently at the screen. Nate looked at the picture and wondered if the thing could see him.

"Ganga nee aaahgrar S'pugh?" demanded the alien.

Nate quickly switched it off again. This thing could be a homing device. The aliens might beam him up. He tossed the gadget across the room; it hit the closet door and lit up again. Nate jumped under the covers and tried to make himself look very small.

Nothing happened. After a few minutes, he peered out from under the blanket. The thing lay on the floor, glowing with the character screen again. Maybe it was like a cell phone directory. Nate crept out of bed and retrieved the device. He tried pushing a different button this time. A new picture appeared; a green-tentacled alien, apparently one of Frazz's species, was wiping away the message Lunchbox had slobbered. Suddenly it jumped back; its eyestalks waved toward the screen. Its wrinkled mouth moved on its belly.

"*Goojat snizzle!*" exclaimed the alien.

Nate tried to remember the alien words he'd learned. "Uh . . . *froonga*? *Plookie*?" The grayish green alien waved its eyestalks wildly and babbled something at someone or something offscreen. Nate switched the communicator thing off again.

I probably said something really rude, thought Nate. Two different aliens. Are they on two different ships? Good guys and bad guys? Or are they all bad? Lunchbox must be on the ship with the Frazz-type alien . . . but he'd been beamed up with the yellow ones. That green one and the yellow ones must be working together. They shot Frazz and Lunchbox . . . so I'll just assume they're all bad. *Game play, world save.* What game? Do the aliens want to play?

Another thought scratched at his mind. Naah, that's stupid. They'd have to be more sophisticated than that. . . . Well, maybe not. What have I got to lose?

Nate quickly stripped off his pajamas and got dressed.

21

razz slumped onto the floor of the cargo bay. Grun-floz limped over to him.

"Good job. You've survived all the way to the intermission."

"If you can call it surviving." Frazz groaned. "Even *you* never beat me up this bad."

"It's not over yet," said Grunfloz. "Your last insult brought us within ten points. I thought it was pretty original—calling Oogash a 'slime-covered refugee from a phlegm jar.' I didn't know you had it in you. We can still win this thing."

"If you recall, I've called *you* that on more than one occasion."

"But still, it was good." Grunfloz gave Frazz an affectionate shove.

"Ow! And no, we can't win this thing. Even if we win the game, they're still going to kill us."

"If I can whip Oogash one last time, I'll die happy."

"That makes one of us. Why is *that* more important than your *life*?"

"It's not. But if we're left with no choice, I prefer to go out a winner. Oogash can never ask for a rematch if I'm dead."

"I'd have to say we're left with no choice," rasped Frazz. "I just wish . . . I just wish that I could eat some of that delicious off-world *froonga* one more time."

"Last meal, coming up," said Grunfloz. He stretched his tentacle out to grab a *froonga* brick that had fallen nearby. "Enjoy. Maybe I'll have one myself." He grabbed a few more from the floor and distributed them evenly between himself and Frazz.

"That's *officers' froonga!*" shouted Oogash from across the cargo bay. "Drop it now!"

The Hoofonoggles lumbered toward them, snarling. The one with two mouths—Frazz couldn't remember their names anymore—roared at him in perfect two-part harmony.

"Aww, blow it out your auditory nubs, *double-drool!*" With nothing left to lose, Frazz threw a *froonga* brick at the mutant. It flew into P'lak's left mouth and lodged in his throat. He staggered back, choking, while his other mouth screamed Hoofonoggle curses.

"You're not nice," translated the computer. The gravity generator shut off again and the game resumed. "Possession, Team Grunfloz."

"Hey, *double-drool*—another good one!" shouted Grunfloz, slapping Frazz on the back and sending him spinning. "You got us the ball!" He snatched the *bzzt*-ball from the air and hurled it at the choking Hoofonoggle, who was turning from yellow to blue. It struck him on the head and stuck there, delivering a powerful jolt. S'pugh's body stiffened, and he floated there, both mouths open, his eyes staring at the Scwozzworts in surprise.

"It worked!" shouted Frazz. "You stunned him!"

"Must be the *froonga*! Hurry! Get to the—*ooof!*—goal!" Grunfloz gleefully slammed P'lak into the wall.

"That's why they don't eat *froonga*! They *can't*!" Frazz zipped past S'pugh's slashing grasp and around Oogash, who was staring at the rigid Hoofonoggle across the room in disbelief. He wrapped his tentacle around the handle of the insult pad and let out the first thing that came to his mind.

"If Hoofonoggles ate *rurfroo*, they'd be cannibals!"

"Insult disallowed," said the computer flatly. "Hoofonoggle cannibalism is a known fact. No points, Team Grunfloz."

"What? Wait, no, I meant—" Frazz took a jolt from the zapper end of Oogash's *whomp-sting* stick.

"Three points, Team Oogash."

Frazz shook himself alert again. "You *gargafron*!"

"You've already used that one," snorted Oogash. *"Malfurbum gwealfee!"*

"That does it, now I'm *really* mad!" Frazz swung the flat end of his stick and cracked Oogash right between

the eyestalks. The impact sent both of them flying in opposite directions.

"For Scwozzwortia!" shouted Grunfloz, deflecting the *bzzt*-ball into the semidazed Oogash. "For *Froonga* Planet!"

"For officers' *froonga*!" Getting his bearings again, Frazz opened up the throttle on his thruster belt and shoved Oogash into the ceiling, pinning him there. He could feel Oogash's muscles starting to relax. "Hurry, Grunfloz! He's waking up!"

"I'm on it!" Grunfloz grabbed the insult handle. "Boil-picking *droob*-fly larva!"

Ding! "Five points, Team Grunfloz."

"*Grrraaaaaaaah!*" Oogash pushed Frazz away and retrieved his floating *whomp-sting* stick. "You'll never win this one! S'pugh! P'lak! Flying wedge! Now!"

Frazz snatched a pair of floating *froonga* bricks. Oogash had the ball and was aiming it at Grunfloz, leaving the Hoofonoggles to block Frazz's path. Frazz hovered until the last moment, and then crammed the bricks into P'lak's right mouth and S'pugh's only one—which was big enough to swallow his whole tentacle. "Eat *froonga*, you *narf*-brains!" Frazz held the bricks there, trying to shove them down the gagging creatures' throats. They clawed at him, but he refused to let go. Grunfloz dodged the *bzzt*-ball, zooming over to assist Frazz with his *whomp-sting* stick. Grabbing Frazz's drifting stick with his other tentacle, he jabbed both of the Hoofonoggles into rigidity. The ball whizzed around and returned to zap Oogash as fast as he had thrown it.

"Okay, Frazz, *triple play*!" shouted Grunfloz. With his tentacles still in the Hoofonoggles' mouths, Frazz fired his thruster while Grunfloz went after Oogash.

Slam! Bam! Thud! Whoosh!

"Tonsil-sucking nostril reamers!"

Ding! "Triple play. Fifteen points, Team Grunfloz."

Oogash roared in fury, and the game escalated into high gear. Each team answered scores with more scores, but weakened by the *froonga*, the Hoofonoggles were no longer invulnerable to the *bzzt*-ball.

Wham! "Hey, P'lak! Is that your head or is your neck blowing a snot-bubble?" *Ding!*

Thud! "*Hnooor sshslossssig zagip flooghaaaaah!*"

"I think you're putting on weight." *Ding!*

Bzzzzzt! Whack! "*Trewhonkian* mud-sniffer!" *Ding!*

Crunch! "*Phronz grglt shavoooolahhh!*"

"I know you are, but what am I?" *Ding!*

Ooooofff! "Everyone said you looked like your mother—so she had corrective surgery!" *Ding!*

"We're winning, Grunfloz! We're winning!"

Beep! The communication panel lit up. Commander Narzargle's voice crackled through it.

"Oogash! I need you on the bridge immediately!"

"But, sir!" Oogash panted. "I can't! I have to score one more—"

"No more playing around!" shouted Narzargle. "Get up here! *Now!* That creature is loose on the ship!"

"I have to win! I can't just let them—"

"That's an order, Oogash! S'pugh! P'lak! Finish the prisoners!"

Oogash clenched his teeth tightly, his head tendrils turning bright orange. "Yes, *sssirrrr*," he snarled, and switched off the intercom. "Aaaaaaarrrrrrrgh!" He snapped his *whomp-sting* stick in half. Placing a tentacle tip on his own goal, Oogash hesitated, and then belched, "Abort game."

As the gravity generator engaged, lowering everything to the floor, the goal computer beeped.

"Abort acknowledged. Forfeit, Team Oogash. Team Grunfloz wins."

"Yes! Yes!" Grunfloz whooped. He woggled his eyestalks and chanted at Oogash, "Loser, loser, loserrrr!"

Oogash bellowed in rage, smashing the goal unit in a shower of sparks. He yanked the door open and stomped out, barking at the Hoofonoggles as he left.

"You heard the commander—finish them now!"

The Hoofonoggles smiled, advancing on the two Scwozzworts with evil hunger in their eyes.

"Weeee no eeeeeats *froongaaaaah*," hissed P'lak. "You breakfaaaasssssst!"

"Well," squeaked Frazz, holding his now-deactivated *whomp-sting* stick in front of himself. "That was a short-lived victory celebration."

22

Aunt Nelly had fallen asleep in the recliner with a satisfied smile on her face. She was still wearing her crown. Nate wore his warmest clothes, though he decided against the ski mask, remembering where it had been. Snow was beginning to fall outside again. He double-checked his equipment list with the contents of his backpack and made sure that his baseball bat was securely strapped to the side. One more thing! He slipped back to his room and grabbed his boom box. Moving quietly across the hardwood floor in his wool socks, he opened the back door, hoping the draft wouldn't make its way to the living room and wake Aunt Nelly, and put his boots on the snow-covered porch before stepping into them. He waited a few seconds after the door clicked shut to make sure he hadn't awakened her, then crunched through the backyard, out of the gate, and onto the sidewalk.

I can't do this at home, he reminded himself as the cold wind sliced through him. It would put Aunt Nelly in danger if it backfired.

When Nate got to the loading dock door, he set the boom box down with the power on. He took off one of his gloves in case he needed to hit the PLAY button immediately. With his other hand he carefully pulled the dock door open. Garbage smells drifted through the air. He shined his flashlight into the manufacturing area. Everything looked normal. The dog food machine was still there with the strange alien contraptions hooked up to it. No aliens present. Another thought hit him. *Fruitcake!* He quickly moved the light over to the corner where Stan had parked the wagon. It was still there, piled high with boxes. Nate heaved a sigh of relief. He gathered his equipment and moved cautiously through the factory to the office area.

He set his overstuffed backpack down in the center of his dad's office. A few things were scattered on the desk. Mr. Parker was not a slob, so Nate assumed the aliens had rummaged through some of his stuff. He unpacked his gear—aluminum foil, Darth Vader mask, Christmas lights, alien communication gadget, colored markers.

Then he dragged some cardboard boxes in from the warehouse and went to work.

Lunchbox peered through the vent above the cargo bay. His nose caught the scent of the Hoofonoggles, as well as the big smelly animal and the little whiny one. Though it was difficult to see, there was a lot of commotion. It appeared that the Scwozzworts were throwing *froonga* bricks at the Hoofonoggles; everyone was running around in circles and taking swings at one another with claws, tentacles, and sticks. Noticing that one of them had a lot more arms than before, Lunchbox felt a twinge of jealousy. I should try that, he thought.

"Awwwwwp!" The thing was almost on him! Lunchbox dashed past the vent and hurried toward the main control core. The ugly creature skittered after him.

The tube opened up into a spacious area. The central computer! Hoses and cables snaked from it in all directions. In the dim light it was difficult to read which was which. Lunchbox concentrated on his memory of the ship's schematics learned months earlier. That one . . . it has to be *that* one. He clamped his teeth around the plug and yanked.

The whole ship suddenly lurched at an angle. The *froonga* storage container slid across the cargo bay, pinning the

Hoofonoggles against the wall. Grunfloz raced to the nearest porthole. The planet was growing closer.

"What happened?" Frazz picked himself up off the deck.

"The orbital maintenance thrusters are off! The ship is falling out of orbit!"

"You mean we're going to crash?" cried Frazz.

"No, we're going to burn up in the atmosphere! If there's anything left of the ship, *that's* going to crash!"

"Wonderful. Did I really want to know that?"

"Never mind!" Grunfloz stepped protectively in front of Frazz as the Hoofonoggles pushed their way out from behind the storage unit. P'lak's many eyes took in the view of the planet growing in the portholes. Grunfloz, seeing their fear, suddenly started speaking slowly and distinctly, as if he were a Scwozzwort *larva*-sitter reading aloud at story time. "Hurry . . . Frazz. . . . We must run to the escape pod!"

"What escape pod?" Frazz waddled after Grunfloz, bobbing one eyestalk behind him at the Hoofonoggles, who immediately gave chase. "The ship doesn't ha— *mmph!*"

Grunfloz wrapped a tentacle around Frazz's mouth and dragged him, still speaking slowly. "There's only one . . . in this corridor . . . oh, *looky,* here it is!" Grunfloz yanked open a pair of double vertical doors; the Hoofonoggles body-slammed him out of the way and scrambled inside. With his head-arm, S'pugh yanked the doors hard; as soon as they latched, the scrap-disposal pod rocketed away from the *Urplung Greebly*, glowing as it entered the planet's atmosphere.

Grunfloz smirked and mockingly imitated Narzargle's voice. "'I think you underestimate them, Grunfloz'— *HA!*"

"Now what? We're still going to die!" Frazz knotted his tentacles.

"To the bridge! Come on!"

The two Scwozzworts stumbled along the deck; it shook as the gravity generators struggled to maintain a constant force. Frazz felt like he was going to *rurfroo*.

"So, do you have a plan?"

"I'm making this up as we go!"

"Why am I not surprised?" said Frazz.

They halted just outside the bridge and peered inside. Oogash was frantically trying to pull the ship out of its crash-dive while Narzargle stood in front of the communications panel. Admiral G'ack's angry face filled the screen.

"Whyyyy you no tell usss of thissss?"

"What are you *talking* about?" snapped Narzargle.

"Thisssssss!" G'ack pressed a button and a new image appeared on the screen, one of entire fleets of spaceships being blown to smithereens. A few fighters destroyed an enormous space station the size of a small moon.

"I have no idea what this is! We had scanned that

planet's defenses repeatedly—didn't we, *Oogash?*" Narzargle turned angrily to his first officer.

"Sir, I'm a little busy right now!" shouted Oogash as he fought to pull the ship up. "Controls not responding, sir!"

"Well, fix them, you *ninny!*"

"I'm trying, Commander!"

"If you hadn't been so wrapped up in your infantile game you could have been minding the ship's systems!"

Grunfloz moved smugly onto the bridge, followed by Frazz. Narzargle immediately pulled his stun-zapper from its holster.

"I see you've found out what happened the last time this planet was invaded," said Grunfloz loudly.

"Lassssst time?" hissed Admiral G'ack.

"Oh, yes, we saw it on our first visit to this place. The invaders never had a chance. We got caught in the crossfire; we were lucky to escape in one piece!"

"Admiral, this is all a *fabrication!*" Narzargle turned bright orange.

G'ack clamped his jaw so tight that one of his lower fangs nearly poked his eye out. "Ssssssshcwossssshworts! You beee on your owwwwwwwwn!" The screen went blank as the ship began shaking more violently. An orange light began to glow around the portholes.

"Oogash!" Narzargle snarled. "Save us!"

"I'm trying!"

"I can fix it, Commander!" Grunfloz moved to the control panel; Oogash shoved him away.

"No! He'll kill us all!"

"I'll kill you myself if you don't move over, Oogash!" Narzargle pointed the stun-zapper. Oogash moved aside but glared at the commander.

"Oogash!" Grunfloz pounded the control panel. "Reroute thruster power to the main engines. Now!"

"How do I do that?" screamed Oogash, holding his tentacles up in panic.

"Stupid *gargafron*," muttered Grunfloz, shoving Oogash. "Get out of my way!" Grunfloz's tentacles flew over the engineering keypad. "Frazz! Get over here and help me out!"

Frazz stumbled over to Grunfloz's side. "What do I do?"

"Take the main power control! You remember how to do that?"

"Of course I do! It's my ship, isn't it?"

"Great. Okay, when I say *go*, pull it back slowly until it's on full. Got it?"

"Got it!"

Grunfloz dashed across the bridge, shoving Narzargle out of the way, and opened the main engine calibration console.

"Okay, Frazz, *go!* Pull!"

Frazz yanked on the lever with both tentacles. It was

still stuck with years of gunk. He tugged harder and it jerked toward him.

"Not so fast! You'll rip the ship in half!"

"Sorry!" Frazz got a better grip on the lever and pulled slowly, while Grunfloz manually readjusted the power input nozzles. The engines slowly thrummed to life. Grunfloz shouted to Narzargle. "Commander! Take the helm! Fire the port nose thruster!"

Narzargle staggered to the helm, grimaced, and punched the button. The ship's nose pointed up, but it continued falling, spinning as it fell.

"Starboard nose thruster! Now! We need to compensate!"

Narzargle pressed the next button; the ship's spin slowed. Oogash clutched the bulkhead, looking like he was about to *rurfroo*.

"Full power!" ordered Grunfloz. Frazz yanked down on the power lever. The ship felt like it would shake to pieces as the engines roared. The orange glow around the portholes began to subside; gradually the ship's descent slowed.

"Approaching zero velocity," said Grunfloz. "Everyone hang on!"

The *Urplung Greebly* suddenly shot upward through the atmosphere. The gravity generators failed to compensate for the inertia; Frazz slid backward into the bulkhead, unable to maintain his grip on the power lever. He felt like a dozen *flarmgroks* had suddenly sat on him, and he strained with his tentacles to reach the console.

Plastered flat on his back against the main control core, Lunchbox could barely move his head. The disgusting squawky thing was pinned against him, pressing into his ribs. I can't . . . fail . . . now. He pushed with his paws at the creature, trying to peel it away. He managed to roll onto his side. The creature flipped onto its back, kicking its legs as it was pushed flat against the side of the core. Lunchbox's right ear was pressed over his eyes, blinding him. The creature flailed with its claws, catching them on the main systems cable. It yanked hard to free itself and the connector popped out of its socket.

The lights on the bridge went dark; the engines groaned to a stop. The inertial forces slowly subsided until there was no gravity and everyone was floating.

"Aaaaah! Grunfloz! What happened?"

"Don't know. All systems are offline."

The only light came through the portholes. Grunfloz pushed himself toward it and looked at the bright blue surface of the planet. The ship paused in its ascent, and gravity slowly returned, but in the opposite direction. The ship was falling again!

"Way to go, genius!" snarled Oogash in the darkness.

"Aaaaaaah!" cried Frazz.

"Can you restart it?" asked Commander Narzargle.

"Not without a service robot," said Grunfloz. "You didn't happen to pack one, did you? Not that there'd be time anyway." He felt around on the console for the battery-powered emergency light switch.

The four Scwozzworts held their breath as the outside of the ship began to glow again.

Grunfloz turned in the direction he'd heard Oogash's voice come from. "At least I beat you again, loser."

"Oh, shut up!" said Oogash.

Grunfloz found the light switch and flipped it on, just in time to see Oogash crawl to Narzargle's side and snatch his stun-zapper from its holster.

Oogash switched the weapon's power to full. "At least I'll have the satisfaction of seeing you go first," he growled.

Again, the ship lurched, throwing everyone against the bulkhead. The stun-zapper flew from Oogash's grip and clattered against the metal wall.

"Are we blowing up yet?" said Frazz.

Grunfloz looked at the porthole. The glow was diminishing again; everyone became weightless. The *Urplung Greebly* began to rise from the atmosphere once more.

"It's a capture beam! From a Scwozzwort command ship!"

Oogash spied the floating stun-zapper and launched himself toward it. Frazz kicked hard against the bulkhead and slammed into Oogash, knocking the wind out of him and deflecting him into the ceiling, where he bounced around the dome with his tentacles flailing.

Grunfloz whipped his tentacle out and caught the stun-zapper. "Oogash is a festering, scab-sucking, pus-gargling, slime-bog wallowing clump of *reegak* filth and a sore loser! Neener neener!"

"*Ding!* Sounds like a game winner to me." Frazz laughed.

"I was hoping to use that one," said Grunfloz, holding the weapon in the ready position.

"What a stupid game," said Narzargle.

23

"**G**runfloz! How come they've arrested *me*? I'm on *your* side!"

"Well, there was a warrant issued fifteen years ago—just like for them." Grunfloz pointed at Narzargle and Oogash, who, like Frazz, had been restrained and were being led down the gangway by a group of muscular young Scwozzwort security officers. "I'll see what I can do—but first I have to finish locking down all of the leaks on the ship." He watched the group grow smaller in the cavernous docking bay, and then made his way to the bridge, with one tentacle wrapped around a new maintenance robot. After opening the service hatch, he was preparing to slide the machine into the duct when he heard a faint scratching noise. Poking his eyestalks into the duct, he called out.

"Hello?"

"Arroooo!" came the reply. "Arroooo!" The voice grew louder until Lunchbox poked his nose out of the duct. Grunfloz reached in, pulled him out the rest of the way, and hugged him, then rolled him onto his back for a belly rub.

"Hey, friend! Thought we'd lost you—I was just getting ready to send this thing in to find your body!"

Lunchbox wagged his tail and barked excitedly. Grunfloz started to close the service hatch, but he heard something else in the duct.

"Awwwwwp! Eeeeeeep!" A six-legged something-or-other flopped out of the hole and scrambled over to Lunchbox, snuggling up to him immediately. Grunfloz's smile grew even wider.

"Well, I'll be! Ha! A baby Zakronian *glompus*! I *wondered* what had happened to that egg!"

Lunchbox rolled his eyes in exasperation as Grunfloz carefully picked the creature up and caressed it. The *glompus* squealed and thrashed its pointy tail until Grunfloz put it back on the deck. Again it snuggled up to Lunchbox.

"I've heard about these things," said Grunfloz. "They imprint on the first thing they see, even if it's a rock. Congratulations, you're a mother."

"Hrrrrmmmmm," growled Lunchbox.

A thin, regal-looking old Scwozzwort stepped onto the bridge. Grunfloz snapped to attention.

"Ultracommander Snargoth!"

"At ease, Grunfloz. What have you got there?"

"That? Oh, that, sir. A Zakronian *glompus*. Very rare."

"No, I mean the other thing."

"This, sir, is our friend from the planet down there. We owe him our lives."

"You'll explain that in your report, I'm sure."

"Yes, sir. How did you know where to find us?"

"Your transponder signal, of course. Didn't think it would take you fifteen years to activate it, though."

Lunchbox realized that was the thing he'd stepped on in the acid-damaged duct, and wagged his tail.

Grunfloz lowered his eyestalks slightly as he followed the Scwozzwort leader down the ramp. "It's a long story, sir."

Grunfloz looked around the huge docking bay. The wrecked hulls of two Hoofonoggle ships littered the deck nearby. "Holy *fleenboodle*! You had a *battle*?"

Ultracommander Snargoth raised his tentacle reassuringly. "Oh, no, nothing like that, Grunfloz. Our scanners picked up a whole fleet of *Urplung* ships exiting the system at top speed. Communications chatter indicates that something scared the *gruzbunkles* out of them! These two must have collided during their emergency reverse. Those old *Urplung* junkers just don't maneuver too well."

"Believe me, I know, sir." Grunfloz smiled. "I definitely know that."

"Now if you'll excuse me, I've a hearing to attend."

The hearing for the accused trio convened in Ultracommander Snargoth's chambers. Snargoth, looking tired, sat on a raised couch. Two Scwozzwort security officers with stun-zappers stood on either side of their leader. Two more flanked each prisoner, with all of them standing in a semicircle below Snargoth's position.

Snargoth motioned to the guard at his right, who stepped forward and addressed them crisply.

"Commander Narzargle, Deputy Commander Oogash, and Sub-Junior Deputy Accounting Officer Frazz, you are charged with the high crimes of conspiracy, treason, fraud, and a lot of other stuff. You will each be permitted to speak briefly. Commander Narzargle, have you anything to say?"

Narzargle exhaled gruffly. "Frazz is a *malfurbum gwealfee*. He should have never been permitted to become an accounting officer. He's a misfit, and his malicious and deliberate manipulation of the facts has ruined my career." Narzargle folded his tentacles and glared at Frazz. "He set us up."

The guard remained expressionless, as did Snargoth. "Deputy Commander Oogash?"

"What he said," rumbled Oogash. "And I would add

148

that Grunfloz was in league with Frazz, and the two of them have conspired to exploit an innocent planet in their selfish quest for *froonga*. Had it not been for our intervention, they might have destroyed an entire civilization."

Snargoth lowered his eyestalks at Oogash. "*Grunfloz* is not on trial here."

The guard waited for a signal from Ultracommander Snargoth, then continued. "Sub-Junior Deputy Accounting Officer Frazz, have you anything to say?"

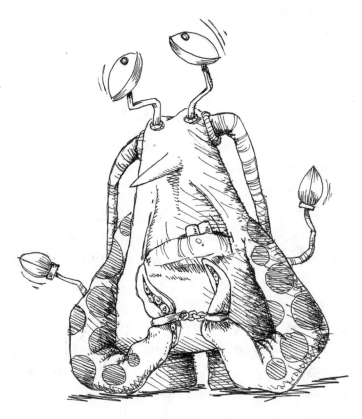

Frazz shuffled his feet uneasily, swallowed hard, and looked up. "Um, well, actually, umm." He took a deep breath and tried not to tremble. "See, it started out when I made this mistake on a sales transaction that—okay, well, at least I was *accused* of making a mistake on this sales transaction, but I don't know exactly if I did or not, but anyway—Commander Narzargle told me I was a *malfurbum gwealfee*, but because the Hoofonoggles were so happy to get all those ships so cheap, well, at least that's what they told me, then I met the Hoofonoggle ambassador who gave me this Medal of Generosity thing, well, at least they told me he was the Hoofonoggle ambassador and I'd never met one, but come to think of it he kind of looked like First Officer Oogash with yellow paint, anyway, they told me I was a hero and made me an honorary citizen and then they promoted me and gave me the *Urplung Greebly* and sent me on a forty-year mission to the middle of nowhere, and then Grunfloz, who was my crew, you know, he picked up a bunch of life form specimens from all over the galaxy because it was his hobby even though he was really sent to spy on me, and all of his specimens got loose and ate our *froonga* and then Grunfloz taught one of the creatures on this planet how to make *froonga* and it was *really good*, but even though they almost blew the planet up, the creatures kept making *froonga* because apparently this one kind of creature really likes it, and then we left and I sent my report to Commander Narzargle—"

"That's enough!" snapped Snargoth, who had been leaning wearily on his tentacle and trying to keep his eyes from glazing over.

"—and then . . . well you know the rest, I think . . . sir." Frazz looked around uneasily. "I didn't mean to babble, sir, it's just that—"

"Shut up!" barked Snargoth. Frazz backed up sheepishly, his head tendrils turning orange. The ultracommander stared at him silently for several minutes, scrunching his wrinkled lower lip up and down several times while he thought.

"You're an *idiot*," he said, and then clamped his mouth shut for another moment. "But you're no *malfurbum gwealfee*." He motioned for the guards to release him and waved him away. Turning to Narzargle and Oogash, he smiled grimly. "But as for *you two* . . ."

Grunfloz paced in the corridor outside Snargoth's chambers. When the door popped open, he heard Narzargle and Oogash wailing in horror. Frazz danced out into the corridor, as giddy as a *fooznak* after a lobotomy.

"What happened?" said Grunfloz urgently.

"Grunfloz! It's wonderful! I'm an *idiot*!" Frazz slapped him on the back and continued dancing and whooping down the corridor.

A guard stepped into the doorway. "Grunfloz, Ultracommander Snargoth will see you now."

24

Nate pushed the mask onto the top of his head and exhaled nervously. He'd been playing his alien invasion video game and science fiction DVD excerpts for hours, occasionally pausing to cackle maniacally through his voice-distortion toy. He looked at the foil-covered cardboard he'd erected around his dad's computer, and the Christmas lights blinking. If he were an alien, would he be dumb enough to believe this was a spaceship bridge? He turned to look at the alien communicator that he'd balanced on the conference table behind him. The screen was blank. The last thing he'd seen before blowing away the virtual mother ship was the yellow creature's eyes. Not really knowing how to read alien expressions, he could only guess that it was scared—at least he could hope.

Something in the warehouse went *bump*.

Nate jumped up and turned the lights off, brandishing his baseball bat and flashlight. With his heart pounding in his ears, he parted the blinds on the warehouse window. He couldn't see anything. Had the yellow aliens found him?

Trembling, he slipped into the hall and turned the doorknob. The hinges squeaked; the sound was like an ice pick through his ear. He opened it just wide enough to slip out into the factory. His boots creaked on the cement floor. He couldn't hear anything except the wind outside. Moving to the wall switch, he turned on the lights.

Nate stopped and held his breath. He thought he heard a squishing sound behind the machine. Nothing! Trembling, he took another breath and held it. One step . . . slowly . . . two steps . . . he leaped around the corner and brandished the bat. Still nothing! The winter wind rattled the corrugated roof of the building. Nate calmed himself. It must have been the wind. He glanced around the building again. Pallet wrapper, check. Dog food machine, check. Alien equipment, check. Decorated wagon, check—uh-oh! The wagon was empty! Nate froze in his tracks as he heard the squishing sound again. He looked at his shadow on the floor in front of him. Another shadow slowly engulfed it.

He started running before he even looked back. It was about eight feet high. Shredded remnants of fruitcake boxes were stuck all over it, as well as bits and pieces of garbage. Nate screamed and ran to the storage section of the warehouse, where pallets of dog food were stacked on steel racks. He kicked his snow boots off and climbed up the cold metal, still clutching the bat. At the top of the rack, he dug in his pocket for his cell phone and dialed 911. The fruitcake monster paused to suck up a bag of dog food that had spilled onto the floor, then sloshed toward Nate. Nate backed farther down the row of pallets, shouting frantically into the phone.

"Help! A giant fruitcake is attacking me! And it's *hungry!*"

The emergency operator sounded annoyed. "Listen, kid, this ain't April Fools' Day."

"I'm serious! My great-aunt baked a bunch of fruitcakes and they're alive, and—hello? Hello?"

Nate snapped the phone shut in frustration. He was on his own. The monster blobbed up to the edge of the racks, trying to suck through the wrapping on the pallets. Unable to penetrate the plastic, it stretched itself higher and higher, until it was only a few feet below him. He gripped his baseball bat tightly. It wouldn't get him without a fight!

The fruitcake thing extended a narrow piece of itself to the top of the pallet. Nate didn't know if it could see him or hear him or just smell him, but it seemed to know where he was and snaked toward him. He raised his bat and struck the tip, then recoiled in horror as the thing pulled the bat out of his hands and absorbed it.

Nate scrambled back as far as he could, pinned between the wall, the ceiling, and the advancing fruit-cake, which now had pulled itself all the way onto the top and flattened out toward him. He threw his gloves off and grabbed at the network of steel cables and braces that supported the ceiling. Pulling himself hand over hand, he climbed away from the stack of pallets and out over the warehouse floor, where he found himself dangling twenty feet above the concrete in his wool socks.

His raw fingers began to go numb from the cold and the hard metal. He had no more strength in his arms to swing himself any farther. The giant fruitcake splooshed off the pallets and slid under him. It stretched upward again. Nate tucked his knees up to his chest, but he knew he couldn't hold them there for very long. His arms felt like they were going to rip out of his shoulders at any second. The fruit-cake stretched until it could almost pull his socks off.

Suddenly a bright flash lit up the walls in the factory, though it did not seem to distract the fruitcake. Nate heard footsteps and voices, but he couldn't make out what they were saying.

A familiar voice suddenly broke the air. "Barrrooooo! Barrrooooo!"

"Lunchbox!" shouted Nate.

Lunchbox dashed between the rows of equipment and pallets. Nate dangled from the ceiling with the fruitcake swiping at his feet. Lunchbox barked more furiously, even getting close enough to the fruitcake to nip at its base. The fruitcake lowered itself and moved toward him. He backed up, still *arrooo*-ing, until it was a good thirty feet away from Nate.

Frazz ran into view, carrying a tubular object of some sort.

"*Naaaaate,*" he shrieked. He raised the object and pointed it at the fruitcake. Another alien, much bigger but the same species, lumbered into view. It grabbed the tube from Frazz and turned it around the other way before raising a similar object of its own.

"*Moomgah!*" bellowed the big alien. Sizzling beams of energy shot into the fruitcake. Gobs of candied fruit, nuts, garbage, and batter sprayed from the monster. The aliens adjusted their weapons and fired again. More intense beams penetrated the thing. It began to smoke and sizzle, melting in places, flaking apart in others. Suddenly it exploded into thousands of tiny chunks, which landed with soft plopping sounds throughout the factory.

Nate felt his grip weaken further; he could hold on no longer.

"*Aaaaaaaaah!*" He watched the floor rush up to meet

him. Two huge green tentacles suddenly whipped out and caught him. Nate looked up to see two slimy eyes staring at him. The big alien gently set him on his feet and stepped back.

"Arroooo!" Lunchbox barreled into Nate, knocking him over, and slurped him repeatedly. Nate hugged him tightly, then adjusted his glasses and looked up at the two aliens. Frazz was smiling—at least Nate assumed that was the way they smiled. The big alien grunted and dipped its eyestalks toward him.

"Umm . . . thank you," said Nate. "I think."

Another series of bright flashes lit up the loading

dock, and within minutes the plant was swarming with green aliens, who began dragging in huge containers of equipment. Others began cleaning up the mess of splattered fruitcake.

Lunchbox sniffed one of the smoldering chunks. *Now it's soft enough for froonga!*

25

Nate heard his parents' voices in the office hallway.

"Personally, Connie, I think that convention was a big waste of time and money. We didn't do anything except fend off questions about how we make our product."

"Well, at least we can say we've been to Chicago."

"I don't know if I can handle the stress anymore. All this talk about space aliens, garbage, a weird machine built by a dog—and still no way for production to keep up with sales. What do I tell the board of directors?"

"We'll worry about it after Christmas, Gerry. Let's just see what Nate is so excited about and take him home, okay?"

"Fine. After you, dear."

"EEEEEEEEEEK!"

"Mom! Dad! It's okay!" Nate jumped up from the conference table in his father's office. "They're here to help!"

Mrs. Parker backed out into the hall, biting her knuckles. "Gerry, t-there are big g-green things sitting in your office," she stammered.

Mr. Parker poked his head through the doorway and gasped. Nate grabbed his arm and pulled him in. "It's okay, Dad. Mom! Come in here! They won't hurt you."

"Aliens . . . in my office," croaked Nate's father. "Okay, it's official. . . . I'm nuts."

"I'll . . . I'll just wait out in the car, Gerry, and, umm, j-just have a nervous breakdown."

"Mom!" Nate ran after her and grabbed her sleeve. "Come on! This is important!" Nate led his protesting mother back into the office, where she cowered behind her husband, who cowered near the door.

Nate pointed to the aliens, who were enjoying a stack of green dog food bricks at the table.

"Mom, Dad, this is Frazz, and this is Grunfloz. We just made a deal." At the mention of their names, the aliens looked up and wiggled their eyestalks.

Mr. Parker's eyes widened, something one might have not thought possible, as they were already as big as pan pizzas. "You made . . . a *deal*?"

"Subject to your approval, of course. I figured a fifty-fifty split was fair."

"A fifty-fifty—Nate, *what are you talking about?*"

"It's simple. We give them half of what we make."

"Half of the *money*? What would aliens want with *money*?" A vein throbbed on the side of Mr. Parker's head.

"No, half of the *froonga*," said Nate, very matter-of-factly.

"Froo . . . what?"

"Dog food. That's their word for this stuff. You can see they really like it." Nate smiled as Grunfloz crammed another brick into his gaping mouth.

Mrs. Parker pointed a shaking finger at Frazz. "Gerry, it's wearing my coat! *My* fur coat!"

"He was cold," said Nate. "Apparently it doesn't snow on their planet."

"*Half* of our dog food?" said Mr. Parker. "Nate, we can't do that!"

"Sure we can. Lunchbox helped translate the contract."

Nate's parents were so shocked to see the aliens that they hadn't noticed Lunchbox sitting at the computer with his oversize keyboard and a strange-looking square thing with alien-looking characters all over it.

"Lunchbox . . . contract . . . but he can't *spell!*" Mr. Parker looked even more dazed.

"Well, I helped. It took us all day. Sit down, Dad. You too, Mom." Nate pulled two chairs out for them. "We have to finish the paperwork so they can get back into space with the first batch."

Grunfloz swallowed his *froonga* and belched. Mrs. Parker clamped her hand over her mouth.

"Frooooongaaaa goooooooood," rumbled the smelly alien.

"T-they speak English?" Mrs. Parker choked.

"No, but we're working on it. Lunchbox understands *their* language."

"Puh . . . paperwork?" said Mr. Parker.

Nate slid a stack of freshly printed papers in front of him. Mr. Parker read out loud, mumbling as he went. "This hereby certifies that the undersigned, Gerald Parker, hmm hmm herfter rfrrd tooz przdntoverth— *PRESIDENT OF EARTH?*"

"We're trying to keep it simple, Dad."

"But I'm *not*—"

"*They* think you are," said Nate, pointing to the aliens. "Lunchbox told them you were the boss."

"But, Nate, I—"

"Look, Dad, do you really think we can go to Washington or wherever and have *them* make a deal with these aliens?"

"Okay." Mr. Parker sighed. "Fine, I'm *President of Earth.*"

Mr. Parker took off his overcoat and loosened his tie. He picked up the contract and continued reading. Mrs. Parker leaned as far away from Grunfloz's breath as possible and read the contract with him.

"'The president of Earth will provide all garbage and manual labor to manufacture Parker's Power Pooch Pellets, aka *froonga*, with the sum total of half of all manufactured product'—did you write this, Nate?—'to be delivered to agents of the Shwo—Scwozzzz'—*what?*"

"*Scwozzwort* home planet," said Nate. "I can't pronounce what they officially call it."

"Nate, we can't *give* them half. We can't make enough of the stuff as it is! We'll go bankrupt!"

"Keep reading, Dad."

Mrs. Parker traced her finger along the next line. "Gerry, it says they'll provide enough equipment and technology to meet the demands!"

"It does?" Nate's dad scanned the contract. "It does!"

"*That's* the coolest part!" said Nate. He jumped up and opened the blinds on the window to the manufacturing area.

Nate's parents gasped in shock. Then they ran from the office into the warehouse. Four enormous, gleaming, fifteen-foot-high alien machines, along with Nate and Lunchbox's original machine, stood neatly arranged in the production section. Two hundred pallets of dog food, completely wrapped, were stacked in the storage area ready for shipping.

Nate eased alongside his parents. "They have their own power source. Lunchbox has calculated that we'll be able to increase production a thousand percent while cutting our overhead in half. Frazz and Grunfloz will handle all the regular maintenance when they come to pick up their shipments. Oh, and they prefer the bricks to the bite-sized chunks."

"Nate, how am I going to explain this to the board? To the *employees*?"

"I don't know, but I'll let you figure that one out. The aliens will only come late at night on weekends, so don't schedule anyone for overtime then."

"You . . . you haven't told any of this to Aunt Nelly, I hope."

"She's as clueless as ever."

Mr. Parker sniffed the air. "Why does it smell like . . . *burned fruitcake*?"

Frazz and Grunfloz stood at the door to the loading platform. The *Naaaaate*-thing, along with the president and first mate of *Froonga* Planet, stood at attention while Frazz faced Lunchbox and made a short formal speech.

"As recently reinstated captain of the newly recommissioned *froonga* transport ship *Urplung Greebly*, and on behalf of the new Scwozzwortian *Froonga* Federation, I present to you, our alien friend, for valor and heroism and all of that other stuff, the Medal of Generosity." Frazz bent down and tied his once-prized possession around Lunchbox's neck.

Nate and his parents applauded, in spite of having no clue what the alien had just said.

"Connie, we must be insane," muttered Mr. Parker.

"Absolutely," she said, and squeezed his arm.

"Naaaaate," said Frazz. *"Flurzobble."* He bowed ceremoniously. Nate bowed back, assuming the alien had just thanked him.

"We should give *them* something," said Nate. "I mean, besides the dog food. A Christmas present, maybe."

Lunchbox perked his ears up and ran back into the office. He returned momentarily carrying a large rectangular object by its handle. He presented it to Grunfloz and wagged his tail happily.

"My boom box!" cried Nate. "He can't—"

"We'll get you a new one," said Mr. Parker. "By all means, let them take it."

"Please," added Mrs. Parker.

"Arf!" said Lunchbox.

The aliens folded their tentacles politely and stepped onto the dock. Grunfloz took a small device from his belt, grunted into it, and both were yanked into the sky by a bright light.

The three humans and their dog blinked and rubbed their eyes for a minute.

Mr. Parker clapped his hands on Nate's shoulders. "Great job, son." He locked the roll-up door, which had been repaired by the aliens.

"Merry Christmas, Dad," said Nate. "Let's go home before Aunt Nelly bakes something."

"Good idea."

With that, the president of Earth led his family out of the building and into the snowy twilight.